RETURN OF THE MONARCHS (AN AMISH ROMANCE)
INCLUDES AMISH RECIPES AND READING GROUP GUIDE

BETH WISEMAN

© 2023 by Elizabeth Wiseman Mackey. All rights reserved. No portion of this book may be reproduced, stored in a retrieval system, or transmitted in any form or by any means—electronic, mechanical, photocopy, recording, scanning, or other—except for brief quotations in critical reviews or articles, without the prior written permission of the publisher.

Published in Fayetteville, Texas, United States.

Cover Design: Elizabeth Wiseman Mackey

Note: This novel is a work of fiction. Names, characters, places, and incidents are either products of the author's imagination or used fictitiously. All characters are fictional, and any similarity to people living or dead is purely coincidental.

To my readers. Thank you for traveling on this amazing journey with me.

ACCLAIM FOR OTHER BOOKS BY BETH WISEMAN

The House That Love Built

"This sweet story with a hint of mystery is touching and emotional. Humor sprinkled throughout balances the occasional seriousness. The development of the love story is paced perfectly so that the reader gets a real sense of the characters." ~ ROMANTIC TIMES, 4-STAR REVIEW

"[The House That Love Built] is a warm, sweet tale of faith renewed and families restored." ~ BOOKPAGE

Need You Now

"Wiseman, best known for her series of Amish novels, branches out into a wider world in this story of family, dependence, faith, and small-town Texas, offering a character for every reader to relate to . . . With an enjoyable cast of outside characters, *Need You Now* breaks the molds of small-town stereotypes. With issues ranging from special education and teen cutting to what makes a marriage strong, this is a compelling and worthy read." ~ BOOKLIST

"Wiseman gets to the heart of marriage and family interests in a way that will resonate with readers, with an intricately written plot featuring elements that seem to be ripped from current headlines. God provides hope for Wiseman's characters even in the most desperate situations." ~ ROMANTIC TIMES, 4-STAR REVIEW

"Wiseman gets to the heart of marriage and family issues in a way that will resonate with readers . . ." ~ ROMANTIC TIMES

"With issues ranging from special education and teen cutting to what makes a marriage strong, this is a compelling and worthy read." ~ BOOKLIST

"You may think you are familiar with Beth's wonderful story-telling gift but this is something new! This is a story that will stay with you for a long, long time. It's a story of hope when life seems hopeless. It's a story of how God can redeem the seemingly unredeemable. It's a message the Church, the world needs to hear." ~ SHEILA WALSH, AUTHOR OF *GOD LOVES BROKEN PEOPLE*

"Beth Wiseman tackles these difficult subjects with courage and grace. She reminds us that true healing can only come by being vulnerable and honest before our God who loves us more than anything." ~ DEBORAH

ACCLAIM FOR OTHER BOOKS BY BETH WISEMAN

BEDFORD, BESTSELLING AUTHOR OF *HIS OTHER WIFE, A ROSE BY THE DOOR, AND THE PENNY* (COAUTHORED WITH JOYCE MEYER)

The Land of Canaan Novels

"Wiseman's voice is consistently compassionate and her words flow smoothly." ~ PUBLISHERS WEEKLY REVIEW OF *SEEK ME WITH ALL YOUR HEART*

"Wiseman's third Land of Canaan novel overflows with romance, broken promises, a modern knight in shining armor and hope at the end of the rainbow." ~ ROMANTIC TIMES

"In *Seek Me with All Your Heart*, Beth Wiseman offers readers a heart-warming story filled with complex characters and deep emotion. I instantly loved Emily, and eagerly turned each page, anxious to learn more about her past—and what future the Lord had in store for her." ~ SHELLEY SHEPARD GRAY, BESTSELLING AUTHOR OF *THE SEASONS OF SUGARCREEK SERIES*

"Wiseman has done it again! Beautifully compelling, *Seek Me with All Your Heart* is a heart-warming story of faith, family, and renewal. Her characters and descriptions are captivating, bringing the story to life with the turn of every page." ~ AMY CLIPSTON, BESTSELLING AUTHOR OF *A GIFT OF GRACE*

ACCLAIM FOR OTHER BOOKS BY BETH WISEMAN

The Daughters of the Promise Novels

"Well-defined characters and story make for an enjoyable read." ~ ROMANTIC TIMES REVIEW OF *PLAIN PURSUIT*

"A touching, heartwarming story. Wiseman does a particularly great job of dealing with shunning, a controversial Amish practice that seems cruel and unnecessary to outsiders . . . If you're a fan of Amish fiction, don't miss *Plain Pursuit*!" ~ KATHLEEN FULLER, AUTHOR OF *THE MIDDLEFIELD FAMILY NOVELS.*

ALSO BY BETH WISEMAN

Contemporary Women's Fiction
The House that Love Built
Need You Now
The Promise

Daughters of the Promise Series
Plain Perfect
Plain Pursuit
Plain Promise
Plain Paradise
Plain Proposal
Plain Peace

Land of Canaan Series
Seek Me With All Your Heart
The Wonder of Your Love
His Love Endures Forever

Amish Secrets Series
Her Brothers Keeper
Love Bears All Things
Home All Along

Amish Journeys Series

Hearts in Harmony

Listening to Love

A Beautiful Arrangement

An Amish Inn Series

A Picture of Love

An Unlikely Match

A Season of Change

An Amish Bookstore Series

The Bookseller's Promise

The Story of Love

Hopefully Ever After

Stand-Alone Amish Novel

The Amish Matchmakers

Short Stories/Novellas

An Amish Adoption

The Messenger

Surf's Up Novellas

A Tide Worth Turning

Message In A Bottle

The Shell Collector's Daughter

Christmas by the Sea

Collections

An Amish Christmas Bakery

An Amish Reunion

An Amish Homecoming

An Amish Spring

Amish Celebrations

An Amish Heirloom

An Amish Christmas Love

An Amish Home

An Amish Harvest

An Amish Year

An Amish Cradle

An Amish Second Christmas

An Amish Garden

An Amish Miracle

An Amish Kitchen

An Amish Wedding

An Amish Christmas

Healing Hearts

An Amish Love

An Amish Gathering

Summer Brides

Memoir

Writing About the Amish

GLOSSARY

Aamen: Amen
ach: oh
boppli: baby
daed: dad
danki: thank you
Deitsch: Dutch
Englisch: those who are not Amish; the English language
Gott: God
gut: good
haus: house
kinner: children
lieb: love
maed: girl
mamm: mom
mei: my
mudder: mother
nee: no
Ordnung: written and unwritten rules in an Amish district

rumschpringe: running around time for teenagers, beginning at 16 years old
schweschder: sister
sohn: son
Wie bischt: How are you?
Ya: yes

CHAPTER 1

Thomas picked up his straw hat from the dusty gravel road for the third day in a row, shook it, then placed it back on his head.

"Hey, Amish boy!" The English man, probably around Thomas's age—eighteen—was a tall guy, a few inches taller than Thomas. He wore jeans and a white T-shirt; his blonde hair hung almost to his shoulders. As he tucked his hands in his back pockets, he said, smirking, "Don't you want to take a swing at me?" He chuckled, as did his two buddies who were dressed similarly, one being about Thomas's size, the other a bit smaller in stature. The boy doing the talking had a red scar that ran horizontally above his right eye, visible beneath the sweat beading on his forehead.

Thomas began walking along the edge of the road that led to his house. His leg didn't hurt anymore, but he still limped from the accident. He hoped he would have his buggy back soon so he could blow past these guys and leave a plume of dust in his wake. But he also had to purchase a new horse. Molly hadn't fared as well as Thomas when the car struck them over a month ago. The mare had survived, but she would never be able to pull a buggy or plow again.

"He's not going to do anything, Rob." The tallest of the three snickered. "Just like he didn't do anything the last couple of times he crossed our paths. They're passive."

Thomas picked up his pace, hoping the three Englishers would go back to doing whatever they were doing instead of standing by the road in the middle of nowhere. They were old enough to drive a car, and they didn't seem to have any purpose being there.

When two hands slammed against his back, hard enough to drop him to his knees, he trembled with rage, but stayed down for a few seconds before he stood and began to walk again. They likely wouldn't do much as he passed by the small general store on the opposite side of the road. Thomas had a sick thought. Maybe they were planning to rob Herron's General Store. There wasn't much else within a half mile or so, only the Byler's place and The Peony Inn, both tucked far off the road. Montgomery, Indiana was a small town with a sizable Amish population, and Thomas's family often did business with members of the community who weren't Amish. He wasn't sure where these three guys lived or came from, but they were more aggressive today. They'd only slung vulgarities his way the past couple of days.

Back on his feet, his right leg throbbed, the one with a pin inside near his knee.

The three guys sped up until they were in front of him, blocking his way. Thomas stopped, facing them as sweat pooled at his temples, and an inner rage boiled as hot as the searing sun. "Don't you have something better to do?"

The small guy folded his arms across his chest as the crook of his mocking smile rose on one side. "Not really. Where's your horse and buggy anyway?"

Thomas didn't want to talk about the accident. "Look, I don't want any trouble. I'm just walking home from work." He wasn't sure he would be able to control his temper if the guy hit him. He'd never been struck in the face, at least not by a fist. Once, a fence post popped loose while he was making repairs and bruised his face, but he'd never been punched.

But it was coming. The short guy stepped forward, clearly unintimidated by the fact that Thomas was taller and more muscular. Maybe all three guys were going to jump him at once. Would he fight back? Would God forgive him? Would he forgive himself?

The tallest of the trio eased his friends to the side. "Arnie, Jeff . . . step aside. I'm the same size as this punk. It needs to be a fair fight."

Thomas looped his thumbs beneath his suspenders, blinking away sweat that was getting in his eyes. "What exactly are we going to fight about? I don't even know you."

"Cuz you live like backwoods trash. Your kind steals jobs away from our families." He poked a finger on Thomas's chest, which fueled his desire to knock this guy out.

"Yeah . . . your father recently outbid Jeff's dad on a big construction job." He nodded to the middle-sized guy. "You're literally taking food off our table. Seems you should stick to working for your own people and stay away from us normal people."

The speaker appeared to be Arnie, which meant the middle guy was Jeff, but he didn't know the name of the person facing off with him. And, for some reason, it became an important detail.

"What's your name?" Thomas lifted his chin a bit higher and adjusted his expression to hide the bubble of fear rising to the surface.

The guy laughed, glancing back and forth at Arnie and Jeff. "I'm about to put my fist in this jerk's face and he wants to know my name?" He shrugged, sporting a Cheshire cat grin. "Sure. I'll tell you my name. Brian Edwards." An eyebrow above his left eye rose. "Ring any bells?"

"As in Edward's Construction?" Thomas wasn't sure why anyone in the Edwards' family would care about losing a bid to Thomas's father. They were a wealthy family by all comparisons, and if the other two were friends of the family, Thomas doubted his family was taking food off any of their tables.

"That would be correct." He nodded to Arnie and Jeff. "All three of our fathers do the construction around here." He snickered. "Well, they hire grunts to do it. They don't have to swing any hammers like I'm sure your old man does."

Thomas was proud of their family business and the way his father had worked to build it into a notable success. They weren't rich and tried to live a simple life, but Thomas worked hard alongside his father, who was still at work on the job now. Thomas left early each day to get home to feed and tend the animals. He'd never minded the mile long walk before a couple of days ago.

Based on the conversation, Thomas was starting to feel like they'd sought him out intentionally. "*Ya*, well. Get on with it then. You know I'm not going to hit you back. I'm guessing this is some sort of warning for us not to offer up any construction bids if you're bidding too."

Brian rubbed his stubbled chin. His hair was dark and parted to one side, a bit more clean-cut than Arnie and Jeff. "I admit, it's irritating when we lose a job to your father, but this is more about . . ." He lowered his head, sighed, then looked up grinning. "We just don't like your kind. I mean, it's weird. The way you live. No electricity, no cars . . ." He pointed to Thomas's black slacks, short-sleeved blue shirt held up with suspenders, then nodded to his straw hat. "And the stupid way you dress."

"You have a right to your opinion, but that doesn't give you the right to instigate a fight." Thomas was sure he wasn't going to win this debate, and he could already see his mother and two sisters fussing over him when he came home with a black eye, busted lip, broken jaw, or whatever else Edward's punch might inflict.

"Whoa—instigate—a big word for a guy who only has an eighth-grade education. Impressive."

Thomas braced himself when he saw Brian curl both fists at his side.

"Just hit him, and let's go," Arnie said. "The girls are waiting at Tina's house."

They all turned toward the general store across the street when the door slammed shut.

"Who's that? Doesn't some older lady run that store?" Jeff asked. "Who's that chick all dressed in black?"

Thomas, like the other three, watched as a girl stomped down the porch steps of the store, then march toward them. If these guys thought he dressed weird, they were going to have a field day with this girl. She had on tight black pants, black boots halfway up her calves, a long-sleeved black shirt that was tucked in and held by a silver belt adorned with tiny silver crosses. A long silver cross hung around her neck. Black tresses of hair fell below her waist, and her eyes cast a shadow on her cheeks as she grew near, her long black eyelashes touching her upper lids. She had a silver ring in her nose and three in one ear. Even her fingernails were painted black.

She stopped in front of their foursome. She couldn't have been much more than five foot tall. Short and skinny. Bright red lipstick covered her full lips. She was sort of pretty, but it was hard to tell with all the dark makeup she wore.

After she slammed her hands to her hips, she said, "Do we have a problem here?"

Something about the way she said it left them all momentarily speechless.

Brian smiled. "No. Not at all. In fact, we're on our way to a little party." He eyed her up and down in a way that left Thomas feeling sick, sizing her up like she was a meal to be devoured. "Care to join us? It's just down the road."

"Don't you have a car?" She presented a flat lipped smile, the kind he'd seen his sisters flash when they were mad, not a real smile.

"We all have cars," Brian said. "But we wanted to stop

and talk to our friend, so we decided to walk today." He nodded to Thomas, who wasn't even sure if these guys knew his name.

She smiled the not-so-real smile again and pointed over her shoulder. "Well, that's my car, and I'm driving *my friend* home." She latched on to Thomas's hand and pulled with the strength of someone twice her size.

They were halfway to the car when she turned around. "Brian Edwards, if I catch you bullying any of the Amish around here again, I'll have my father get in touch with yours. Although, I halfway expect he's as big a bully as you." She pointed her finger at each one of them. "As all of you."

Thomas attempted to shake loose of her hand, but he didn't try very hard. She had a firm hold on him, and he'd never held an English girl's hand.

Brian laughed loudly before he shouted back at her. "Coming from someone who dresses like you? Oooh, I'm scared. Shaking in my boots." He held up his hands. "But we'll get on down the road. We have some hot *normal* girls waiting for us."

After Brian, Jeff, and Arnie started walking, the girl abruptly let go of Thomas's hand. "Get in," she said when she opened the driver's side of a sleek black two-door car.

Thomas was still speechless. And humiliated.

After she started the car, she twisted to face him, then extended her hand. "Hi, I'm Janelle."

As he took her hand, she smiled . . . a real smile this time.

CHAPTER 2

Thomas was embarrassed that a girl had to stand up for him, and he hoped Janelle would mistake his blushed face as being from the heat, not total humiliation. He kept his eyes straight ahead as he said, "I just live about a half mile from here. *Danki*—I mean thanks for the ride."

"Those guys are such jerks." She shook her head full of black hair as she shifted her car into gear. Thomas had driven an automatic car a few times. He was in his *rumschpringe*, or running-around period as it was often called by the English. But he'd never even been in a car like the one he was in now. It was a two-seater, rode low to the ground, and had all kinds of gadgets on the dashboard.

He didn't want to focus on what had just happened. "I've ridden by that store hundreds of times, but I've only seen an older woman out front from time to time."

"That's my mom. She's got an unseasonal case of the flu. She seems to get it every year, but usually not in the summer like this. So, I'm running the store until she feels better. I already work there part-time." She tapped her chin. "Depending on when I decide to leave for college, I might stay on and continue to help her for a while."

Now that he was seeing her up close, Janelle didn't look any older than Thomas, maybe even younger.

"How old are you?" he asked. "Don't you have another year or two of high school?" Even though Thomas's people only went to school through the eighth grade, he knew the English were usually eighteen when they graduated.

"I'm seventeen, but I graduated early." She turned to him and smiled. He wanted to ask her why she dressed in black. She wasn't wearing the type of black mourning clothes typically worn by the English.

"You must be really smart," he said as he glanced at her.

Janelle shrugged. "I don't know about that. I just didn't care for school and was anxious to graduate. It's a small town, and I never really connected with any of the kids over the past six months since we've lived here."

Thomas wasn't surprised based on the way she was dressed. He'd never seen any of the English kids here dressed the way she was or wear such dark makeup, especially around her eyes. "Where'd you move from?"

"Not far. Indianapolis. My mom grew up in the country, on a farm near Shoals, and she wanted to get back to her roots even though we don't have any family there or here in Montgomery. But Mom said Montgomery was a hop, skip, and a jump from her old stomping grounds, as she called them. My dad owns his own construction company, and after making some inquiries, he discovered there was plenty of work around here." She turned to him, her dark eyes taking on a glistening glow as she spoke. "My parents are still so in love after twenty-five years of marriage. I'm not sure my dad would deny my mom anything." She chuckled. "I still catch them making out like teenagers when they think I'm not around."

Her voice, ambitions, and sweet nature didn't seem to match the look she had chosen for herself.

"Go ahead. Ask me why I dress like this." She shrugged again as she cut her eyes at him, but with a grin on her face. "Most people are too afraid."

Thomas swallowed back a knot in his throat. He appreciated how candid she was, but wasn't it her business what she chose to wear? It wasn't an option Thomas could adhere to since his people all dressed alike.

"Uh . . . it's okay. I guess it's fine to dress however you like." He wondered if that's why she hadn't made any friends over the past six months. Close up, she looked like she might be pretty beneath the dark makeup.

"Wanna stop for a soda? I'm parched." Even with the air-conditioning blowing in their faces, the car hadn't had time to cool down. "My treat."

"That's *mei haus*, that way." He pointed to the road that led to his home.

"Soda or not?" She didn't slow down.

They passed the gravel road to his house. "*Ya*, sure." He didn't seem to have a choice.

She turned into the parking lot of a small diner about a mile further down the road, put the car in park, then exited the vehicle. Thomas stepped out and followed her.

Inside, Janelle ordered a root beer float, and Thomas ordered the same before they took a seat at a booth in the corner of the small establishment.

"I haven't had one of these in a long time," he said as he slid into the seat and removed his hat. He took a long sip from the straw, absorbing a hefty chunk of whipped cream on top. "It's as good as I remember."

"My dad loves these. My mom can't stand root beer. It's one of the few things they disagree on." She smiled, and again, Thomas thought again about how pretty she would be without all that stuff on her face, but he also wondered if she had an explanation about her choice of clothing and makeup. Maybe he should have asked her when she brought up the subject.

She leaned back and stared at him. "I've seen you drive by in your buggy several times when I was helping my mom or just stopping by the store. Where's your horse and buggy?"

Thomas cleared his throat. He didn't like to talk about what happened, but it was a direct question he couldn't really avoid, especially if he wanted to find out more about her. "I got hit by a car. *Mei* buggy got pretty banged up, and *mei* horse is out of commission permanently, but she's okay. I'm on the lookout for a new horse, and *mei* buggy is getting repaired."

Her eyes were heavy and locked with his. "And you? Is that why you walk with a limp? I mean it's barely noticeable, but I just wondered."

Thomas focused on his drink and avoided her inquiring eyes. "*Ya*, I have a pin in *mei* leg."

She nodded. "People around here need to be more

careful. Everyone knows the buggies have the right-of-way. If I had to guess, someone probably zoomed past you or spooked your horse to cause the accident."

"*Nee*, we were hit from behind." He flinched at the recollection, the crunching of metal against the back of the buggy, the way he was flung from his seat, landing on the gravel road, and the horrific moaning that came from his beloved horse.

"I can see you don't like to talk about this." She sighed as she pulled her eyes from his and took a long sip of her float. Then she leaned forward and found his eyes again.

He held her gaze even though it was hard to distinguish where the dark makeup started and ended since her eyes were practically the same color, a deep dark shade of brown, but with the shadowy makeup, her eyes looked almost black. He couldn't stand it anymore. "So, why *do* you dress like that?"

She grinned before leaning over for another sip, but kept her eyes on him, eyebrows raised. "You first." Her voice was soft and sweet, such contrast to her looks.

His eyes widened. "If you've lived here for six months, I would assume you know that we all dress pretty much the same." He scratched his cheek, surprised how much scruff could develop in one day. His father always said he'd have a fine beard when he was married and allowed to grow one. Right now, it was a nuisance to have to shave every day.

"Of course, I know you all dress the same, have the same haircuts, don't use electricity or drive cars, etc. What I'm asking is the same question you asked me . . . why?"

Thomas wasn't sure he'd ever had to explain this to an

outsider. "That's the way it is, the way it's always been. We follow the *Ordnung*, the rules of the Amish."

"I'm familiar with the *Ordnung* and the rules. But I'm asking for the meaning behind the rules. Why do you all insist on uniform clothing, houses, and everything else?"

Thomas had a feeling she already knew the answers to her questions, which made him wonder if she was setting him up for something. "There's no competition. We're all the same in *Gott's* eyes."

She smiled. "And there you have it . . . the answer to your question about why I dress the way I do. I'm not competing with anyone else. I don't care if other girls have fancy clothes, nor do I feel the need to fit in."

"You sure have a fancy car," he said, grinning.

She chuckled as she nodded out the window to the sleek black car. "Point taken. My dad bought it for me when I turned sixteen."

Thomas stared at her, waiting for more. When she didn't say anything, he asked, "I get the no competition, but why all black . . .?" He raised an eyebrow. "All black, even your eye makeup and fingernails?"

She looked down, her face taking on a blush for the first time, visible even beneath the makeup. "It's not for everyone."

"I didn't say I didn't like it." He didn't, but he didn't want to hurt her feelings. "It's just, you're pretty and you seem to be trying to cover that up."

Her cheeks glowed a brighter shade of red. She lifted her eyes to his. "I know it must seem like I'm hiding, but I'm not. I'm a future butterfly."

"Huh?" Thomas leaned back against the seat the same way she was and scratched his cheek again.

"I know people look at me funny. My parents think it's a stage I'll grow out of, and in some way they're right, but they're right for all the wrong reasons. I'm not being rebellious. I'm not a Goth chick or practicing devil worship and anything like that. I'm evolving, like a caterpillar before it becomes a butterfly."

Thomas was in over his head with this girl's reasoning, but he was intrigued by every word that came out of her mouth. "*Ya*, go on."

She took a deep breath, then held up her left hand. "See these two rings." She wiggled her fingers. The middle two had black rings, each with something silver atop them, something too little for him to see. "One represents the death of my grandmother and the other one the death of my grandfather." She paused, lowered her head for a moment, then added, "I don't feel at peace about their deaths yet. They both died last year, and I didn't get to say goodbye." She shrugged a little. "I will get past it, but I'm not there yet. I'll take them off when I feel peace about their passings."

She held up her right hand and touched a thick black band around her wrist. "I hit a wall in my bedroom when I was mad about something, and this reminds me that violence of any type should be avoided if possible. And until I can control my angry outbursts sometimes, I wear this."

Thomas could see where she was going with this, and he found it interesting, if not odd.

"The black clothes are because I am not the person I

want to be. I strive to be better, and as I grow and change, so will my clothes. And I believe all white should be reserved for marriage." She shrugged. "It's weird, I know, but it's how I feel."

Thomas gazed at her from across the table, trying not to scowl.

"You're staring at my face and wondering about my makeup."

He nodded. "*Ya*, I am."

She wiggled her mouth, covered in red lipstick, back and forth as she fidgeted with her straw. "I don't see the world clearly. I have questions. I want a better relationship with God. I want to understand myself better and what makes me tick. As I grow into the person I want to be, I will lighten my colors. And I feel that overall, about my appearance. I want to represent the version of myself that I see, and as I see changes—for the better I hope—then I will adjust the way I represent myself on the outside. And I don't worry about what people think of my looks or who they perceive me to be."

At some point, Thomas's jaw had dropped, and he was speechless. Although, everything she said made sense and inspired him to care less about the stares he received from the English sometimes.

"My parents aren't crazy about my choices, but they understood once I explained to them. I guess I haven't really made any close friends because no one bothered to get to know the real me. And that's okay. People shine from the inside, and I want to be friends with those who can see my light beyond my outward appearance."

Thomas wasn't sure anyone had shone more brightly in his eyes than Janelle did now.

"I think that's awesome," he finally said before he smiled.

"Really?" She tipped her head to one side before she leaned down and took a sip of her root beer float.

"*Ya*, really. I wish I was more like you. I worry too much about what outsiders think of me, the way I dress, and all the other things you mentioned. I admire your sense of freedom, and you know who you are."

"Not really. I mean, I know who I *want* to be, but I'm not there yet."

"I have a feeling you'll get there." Thomas couldn't stop staring at her, at the real person, the one she hid from the world. But he had one more question. "Why the bright red lipstick?"

Her cheeks began to turn pink. "You probably won't believe this, but I've never kissed anyone." She lowered her head before she looked back at him. "You know, a guy . . . like a real kiss. I'm seventeen so I guess that makes me a little freakish, huh? I'm sure even Amish guys your age have kissed girls by now."

Thomas hesitated since his people didn't usually discuss this kind of thing, but he finally nodded. "*Ya*, I have." Not a lot, but there had been a few. He had thought that each girl might end up being a future wife, or a girlfriend, but he hadn't met anyone that he'd gotten serious with so far.

She straightened. "So, when is your buggy going to be fixed? And you have to get a new horse, right?"

It was jarring the way she changed the subject so

quickly, but he was happy to move in another direction. "I don't know when either of those things are going to happen. I'm on the hunt for a *gut* horse, and *mei* buggy is being repaired now. Luckily, it's only a mile to work."

"And very unlucky that Brian and his goons live nearby. They will probably try to bully you again on your way home."

Thomas had been raised to be passive, but he didn't want to appear a coward to Janelle. "I can take care of myself."

She smiled a little. "I know you *can* take care of yourself, but I also know you don't want to, that it goes against what you believe in. And I lock up about the time you're walking home from work. Just come into the store, avoid those guys, and I'll drive you the rest of the way home."

Thomas felt like she was offering him protection from Brian and his buddies, and no matter how passive he might be, he possessed a certain amount of pride. But if he said no, he might not have an opportunity to spend time with her and getting to know Janelle better had suddenly become a priority. "*Ya*, sure, I guess that would be okay. *Danki* . . . I mean thanks."

She winked at him. "And maybe tomorrow we can change it up and get an ice cream sundae."

Thomas smiled. "Maybe we can." Then he winked back at her as he wondered what was happening between him and his new friend. Was she flirting? Was he flirting back?

He just knew he wanted to get to know her better, and a person could never have too many friends.

CHAPTER 3

Janelle waited for the gate to open, then pulled into her driveway with a bounce in her step. Thomas was handsome, nice, and . . . safe. They'd never have a romantic relationship since he was Amish, so Janelle didn't have to dig into her deepest fears.

She went straight to her mother's bedroom since she'd noticed her father's car wasn't in the driveway. The door was open, so she tiptoed in, surprised to see her mother sitting up and reading a magazine.

"You look like you feel better." Janelle walked to the edge of the bed and sat. Her mom set the magazine aside and reached for Janelle's hand and squeezed.

"I do feel much better. How did it go at the store?" She yawned, covering her mouth with her free hand.

"Pretty good for a Wednesday Not much traffic, but two ladies came in and spent about a hundred and fifty dollars each."

Her mother raised an eyebrow. "Goodness. What did

the ladies buy?" She gently eased her hand away, then tucked her shoulder-length blonde hair behind her ears. Janelle had always thought Sharlene Herron was the most beautiful woman and mom on the planet, inside and out. Maybe it was because she was an only child, but Janelle and her mother had always been close.

Janelle tapped a finger to her chin as she recalled the purchases. "Uh, let's see . . . the taller lady bought two books, three of the candles we had on sale, an angel figurine, and ten jars of jam, the kind Lizzie and Esther make with the Amish labels on them. And the other woman bought books, candles, and . . ." Janelle laughed. "And she bought that horrible red vase shaped like a shoe!"

Her mother's eyes widened. "You're kidding! I was sure we'd have to slash the price on that hideous thing to get rid of it." She shrugged. "To each his own, I guess." She glanced at the clock on her bedside table. "You're a little late today."

"Oh, yeah." She pushed dark strands of hair from her face. "I gave a guy a ride home."

Her mother frowned as she lifted a sculpted eyebrow. "Someone you know, I hope?"

She shook her head. "No, but he was an Amish guy."

"Amish have their own problems and bad eggs like everyone else. It's still not safe to pick up strangers, Janelle."

"I know, but Brian Edwards and two of his friends were giving the guy a really hard time. I watched out the window for a while before I went outside and got him away from them and took him home."

"Why does that name sound familiar, Brian Edwards?"

Janelle reached up and began taking off her black earrings, one pair at a time. Her mother frowned again, but she'd stopped commenting on Janelle's clothing and accessory choices a long time ago. "I think Dad knows his father. Brian is a real bully. I don't really know him, but I've heard stories, and today I witnessed it for myself. He shoved Thomas down, and I knew the poor guy wouldn't fight back."

Her mother shook her head, frowning. "Yes, an unfair advantage for Brian." She glanced at the clock on the nightstand again. "Where does he live?" she asked, clearly referring to the time again.

"Only about a half mile from the store, but we went to that little café and got root beer floats. Thomas is a super nice guy." Janelle liked the way his name rolled off her tongue, and she was lost in the memories of his blue eyes and the way he looked at her. When she snapped out of it, her mother was grinning. "What?" she asked.

"I think I saw some dreaminess in your eyes." She smiled as she batted her eyes at Janelle. "Is he cute?"

Janelle sighed. "Handsome, Mother. At our age, it's handsome, not cute. And, yes, he's very handsome."

"Be careful. He's Amish, and Amish only get involved with their own kind, at least most of the time."

"I know that we'll never be more than friends, and that's okay. I like him, and as you've said before . . . a person can never have too many friends." She half-chuckled. "And even one friend would be nice."

Her mother coughed, blew her nose, then said, "You do this to yourself, Honey. I understand why, but you are beautiful inside and out, though you never let anyone see the real you." She reached for Janelle's hand and squeezed. "Someday you will."

Janelle didn't think so, but she raised one shoulder and lowered it slowly. "Maybe." She felt more comfortable with Thomas than she had with anyone she'd met since they'd moved to Montgomery.

"I think I need at least one more day of rest, then I'll get back to the store. Are you going to stay on part time until you leave for college?"

"Yeah, if it's okay with you. I like working there."

"It's fine with me. I like having you around."

Janelle stood when she heard the front door close. She leaned over, kissed her mother on the forehead, and said, "Ditto," before she left the bedroom.

"There's my beautiful girl." Her father wrapped her in his arms the way he had her entire life. "My beautiful Goth girl."

Janelle sighed before she eased out of the hug. "Dad, I told you . . . no one dresses Goth. I'm just—"

"I know, I know. You're growing from a caterpillar into a butterfly." He rubbed her arm. "I'll be happy to see that butterfly when the time comes."

Janelle forced a smile before she inched around him and toward the kitchen. The whole caterpillar/butterfly thing was real, even though it sounded silly even to herself sometimes. But there was so much more to it.

THOMAS TOOK a seat at the dining room table across from his father while his mother and two sisters scurried around the kitchen. His siblings were probably trying to expedite supper so they could go meet their boyfriends down by the pond. Kathryn was nineteen, and Elizabeth was twenty, and they'd snagged two twin brothers—Abraham and Luke—who looked nothing alike. But the girls were smitten, and Thomas foresaw two wedding announcements in their futures. His sisters had been seeing Abraham and Luke for almost a year.

"What happened to your arm?" His mother frowned as she placed a butter dish on the table and nodded to the scrape on Thomas's forearm.

He glanced at the spot on his arm his mother was staring at. He hadn't even noticed the scratch, but it wasn't worth lying about. "Brian Edwards and two of his friends." Shrugging, he hoped that would be the end of it, but based on his mother's expression, she wasn't going to let it go.

Elizabeth gasped before his mother could question him. "Brian Edwards is a horrible human being." She slapped her hands to her hips. "He's a bully, especially to our kind."

"We don't speak that way in this *haus*, Elizabeth Marie." Lavina Schrock rarely raised her voice, and when she did, the family paid attention. "We don't call anyone a horrible human being." She pointed a finger at Thomas's oldest sister. "During prayer, you need to ask forgiveness for saying such a thing."

Their father cleared his throat. "*Ya*, well . . . if he's anything like his *daed*, he probably is a horrible human being."

His mother groaned. "Eli, you're not helping things."

His father shrugged. "It's true. I know who Brian Edwards is, and I've had dealings with his *daed*, a wretched and spiteful person. He often gets outbid on construction jobs—by me and others in our community—and he's been rather threatening about it. I'm sure that's why his *sohn* targeted Thomas."

"Are you hurt anywhere else?" Apparently, his mother was giving up the battle and refocused on Thomas's arm.

"*Nee*." Thomas shook his head as he reached for a slice of bread on a platter in the middle of the table even though everyone wasn't seated, nor had they said grace. He wouldn't eat it before they prayed. He just wanted to avoid the curious eyes that were waiting for further explanation. Passiveness might be the Amish way, but it was still embarrassing to not be able to stand up for himself when the situation warranted it. "It's just a scrape," he finally said.

His mother and sisters took their seats, and they all bowed their heads in prayer. Thomas thanked the Lord for the food and his many blessings, but he also asked God to keep Brian and his friends out of his way. It had been humiliating to be rescued by a girl.

"Where did this happen?" his mother asked, being the first one to raise her head to speak.

Thomas sighed. "*Mamm*, it's not that big a deal. Brian pushed me down, and him and his friends threw a bunch of rude comments *mei* way. That's all. And it happened across from that little store on *mei* walk home."

"Herron's General Store? I love that place. It's like a combination general store with gifts and food items."

"*Ya*, that's the place." Thomas began to fill his plate

with ham, potatoes, sweet peas, and cucumber salad, willing the conversation to be over.

"Sharlene Herron is a delightful *Englisch* woman. I've been in that store many times." She paused, scowling. "Did those boys give you a hard time the rest of the way home? That store is a half a mile from our *haus*."

Thomas laid his fork on his plate. "*Nee*, they left me alone, and Sharlene Herron's daughter was closing the store, so she gave me a ride home." *Now please let it go.*

"I've seen that *maed* working with her *mamm*." She paused. "She's very nice, like her *mudder*, but she dresses all in black. Even her face is painted with dark makeup." Tipping her head to one side, she waited for Thomas to look at her. "Did she say why she dresses so differently?"

Thomas sighed, frowning. "Why do we dress so differently?"

His father cleared his throat and shot Thomas a warning look. "Careful, *Sohn*."

Kathryn and Elizabeth were practically shoveling their food in their mouths, each glancing at the clock on the wall.

"Those boys will be down by the pond," his father said sternly. "Quit eating this fine meal as if it's your last."

His sisters grinned at each other before both declaring they were done.

"You will stay and help your *mudder* clean the kitchen, like always." Their father cut his eyes at each of his daughters.

"It's all right, Eli. Let them go." She turned to Thomas. "I'd like to talk to Thomas anyway. I don't get to visit with him as much as the girls since they're here all day and he's at work."

Thomas's father would retire to the porch where he'd read the newspaper for about fifteen minutes before he headed to the bedroom. His mother rarely wanted to visit with Thomas, so he figured it was about the girl from the store.

The girls wasted no time rushing to slip into their shoes while Thomas and his parents finished eating.

"And stay where I can see you out this window." Their father nodded over his shoulder to the kitchen window. Thomas—and his sisters—knew that their father could also see them from the porch and his parents' downstairs window. What they didn't know—or maybe they did— was that there was a patch of trees that blocked the view from all the rooms and porch. Thomas was sure that's where the kissing happened after his parents had extinguished their lanterns for the evening. Thomas had heard Elizabeth and Kathryn talking about kissing their boyfriends down by the pond. And it was bound to happen when they went on weekend dates where their father was nowhere around. He'd heard his dad say that he could control what happened on his own property and that he hoped his daughters acted respectfully, and Abraham and Luke too, when they were away from home.

Elizabeth and Kathryn were grown women, but Thomas believed that they acted appropriately, the way they'd been raised—his sisters and their boyfriends.

After his father finished eating and excused himself, his mother dabbed her mouth with her napkin. "What was Sharlene's daughter like? Did you get to talk to her much? As I said, she's always been very sweet, but I don't understand why she dresses the way she does." His mother set a stack of dirty dishes in soapy water, then tossed a dish towel over her shoulder and leaned against the counter, raising an eyebrow as she faced him. "Did she mention anything about that?"

"*Mamm*, does it really matter? She's just a girl who gave me a ride home." Janelle's admissions about her attire had felt personal, and he didn't want to share the information. "We stopped and got a root beer float at the café, and then she brought me home." He cringed when his mother rushed to the kitchen table and sat across from him, her eyes wide. Thomas shouldn't have mentioned that part.

"I saw a car drive away, but I couldn't make out who was in it. Even her car is black. Does she go to the local *Englisch* school?"

"*Mamm*, really? You're grilling me." He narrowed his eyebrows. "But I can see you're not going to let up so here you go . . . you're right, she's a nice person. Her name is Janelle. She's entitled to dress however she likes, and she offered to give me a ride the rest of the way home tomorrow, too, and I'll be happy to accept it since I'm dripping in sweat from the mile walk home. This way, it's only a half a mile." He took a breath. "And she graduated early before they moved here."

His mother rubbed her chin. "Where was Sharlene?"

"Her *mudder* has been sick, but I didn't get the impression it was anything serious."

She tilted her head to one side. "Be careful. There's nothing wrong with having a new friend, but just don't let it develop into anything else." She shook her head. "Although, based on her appearance, I don't see that happening. I think there's a beautiful *maed* underneath all that makeup, but I know she's not your type."

His mom stood and went back to the kitchen sink, seemingly convinced that Thomas and Janelle would never be anything more than friends.

But Janelle intrigued him, and he couldn't wait to see her tomorrow. He couldn't tell his mother his thoughts or that he couldn't stop thinking about her.

CHAPTER 4

Janelle closed the shop right at five o'clock, and just as she was locking up, she heard voices across the street.

"There's the Goth girl!"

She wasn't sure who shouted at her, nor did she care or plan to lower herself to their level. After going straight to her car and starting the engine, she locked the doors, then peered down the street. She could see Thomas in the distance heading her way, so she backed up, and oops . . . slung a little dirt at Brian Edwards and his friends.

"I shouldn't have done that," she said as Thomas got into the car. "Slung dirt at them by spinning my tires. It's just that they are so mean." She peered at the three guys through her rearview mirror as they waved their arms around to clear the dust.

"You didn't have to pick me up." Thomas took off his straw hat and ran a hand through his wet brown hair. Sweat trickled down the sides of his face and beaded on his forehead.

"I thought that was the plan." She offered a weak smile, wondering if he had regretted their semi-date to get an ice cream.

"*Nee*, I mean, I could have walked all the way to your store without you having to back up." He swiped at more sweat on his forehead since her air conditioning hadn't begun to cool the car yet.

All three boys lifted their middle fingers as Janelle drove by them, and though she was tempted to return the gesture, she was pretty sure it would offend Thomas, and she'd feel badly about it later. "Yeah, I think I did have to pick you up." They both knew why, but she shifted the focus and grinned at him. "Because you were already melting from this heat."

He smiled. "*Ya*, I guess so."

She started slowing down when they approached the café. "Still up for a sundae?" Even though she'd thought about Thomas a lot since yesterday, she also worried if maybe she had shared too much. That wasn't like her, to be so open.

"*Ya*, I'm always up for a sundae." He still had his hat in his lap.

She giggled.

"What's so funny?" His mouth crooked up on one side in a half smile.

"Your hat hair." She ran a hand in a circle above her head. "It's all flat."

"Hazards of the way we dress. Lots of hat hair." He smiled a little broader just as she turned into the café.

Inside, they went back to the same booth as before and

each ordered a hot fudge sundae and a glass of water. "Can I ask you something?" He squinted at her.

"Well, I guess so. I probably over-shared yesterday with my whole caterpillar/butterfly story." She already wished she could take it back, especially since it was only partly true.

He lifted a shoulder, dropped it slowly, and held her gaze. "I think it's a cool plan. I'm looking forward to watching you shed your skin." He lowered his head, put a hand to his forehead, and laughed. "*Ach*, wow. That almost sounded nasty. Sorry."

She laughed. "Yeah, shame on you. But a caterpillar *does* shed its skin several times before it becomes a butterfly, spreads its wings, and flies away."

"So . . . *mei* question is . . ." He dipped his spoon into the ice cream but kept his eyes on her. "As I get to know you, are you going to start losing some of your skin? And, you know what I mean . . . shed some black?"

"Maybe." Janelle could only show him so much of herself, and their friendship was only just beginning. At least, she hoped they would be friends.

He swallowed, then dabbed his mouth with a napkin. "I mean, you explained to me about the black clothes, but long sleeves? It's July." He tipped his head to one side, his blue eyes fixated on hers.

She swallowed her ice cream, then took a deep breath, carefully planning her answer. Most people didn't want anything to do with her, so his question wasn't one she had to respond to often. "I just like black, and I prefer long sleeves." She heard the snippiness in her response and regretted it. She liked Thomas, at least what she knew about him so far. In addition to being handsome, he wanted to get to know her. The real her, what was inside. Or so it seemed. "I'm sorry. I didn't mean to sound so snippy. It's just . . ." How could she explain?

"It's okay." He reached across the table and put his hand on hers. It was brief, but Thomas's touch was gentle before he slowly eased away. "You wouldn't believe how many times I've been asked why the Amish dress the way we do. I get sick of explaining it to the *Englisch* all the time, so forget I asked. Really. It's fine." He smiled, then took another bite of ice cream.

Janelle lowered her head and blinked back tears. Only her parents knew her biggest secret, and they had to love her. She wondered what it would be like to have a guy love her.

"*Ach, nee.*" Thomas put his spoon down as his eyes widened. "Please don't cry. Dress however you like. Really."

She wasn't sure why Thomas's opinion of her mattered so much. "Excuse me," she said as she slid out of the booth seat and rushed to the back of the café.

It was a one-person restroom, and after she locked the door, she stared at herself in the mirror. Tears had managed to mingle with her thick black mascara and dark eye shadow, leaving dark rings underneath her eyes, which only made her cry harder.

After continuing to glare at herself in the mirror, crying more, she placed her hand underneath the soap dispenser, mixed the thick liquid with water, then scrubbed her entire face. It took several times of going through the process, but after the final rinse, she dried her face with paper towels. She even wiped off her red lipstick. It was a good long minute before she stopped crying and eyed herself in the mirror, her vision smiling back at her. Maybe Thomas would stop asking questions that she wasn't prepared to answer.

~

THOMAS DIDN'T UNDERSTAND WOMEN. And he felt like a total cad for causing Janelle to cry, especially when he was sensitive to the same questions himself. *Who cares how a person dresses? It's what's inside that matters.*

As he lambasted himself for hurting her feelings, the bell on the door jingled, turning his attention to an older couple coming into the café. But through the window, he saw Brian and his friends lingering around Janelle's car, and his chest tightened. The trio's beef was with Thomas, not Janelle, and he silently prayed they wouldn't damage her car, like running a key down the side of the black paint.

After laughing, Brian, Jeff, and Arnie slowly walked down the street. Brian admitted that all three had cars, so Thomas could only surmise that they were hanging around on the quiet two-lane road just to give him trouble. Maybe he shouldn't have accepted rides from Janelle. He could have unintentionally dragged her into this confrontation that hopefully Brian would forget about soon.

A few moments later, they were out of sight, and Thomas looked over his shoulder toward the restroom. If Janelle didn't come out soon, he would ask the waitress standing behind the counter to go check on her. He liked this place, the 1950s set up with red-seated booths and a soda-type bar that ran the length of the back wall.

He glanced down at his ice cream, which was nearly gone, but Janelle's sundae was slowly melting. Rubbing his forehead, he wondered how he could make it up to her since it was his fault she cried. He couldn't stand to see any girl cry, but his stomach churned even worse because it must have seemed like he was judging her about her clothes, but they'd already been down that road. He just wondered why she didn't wear short sleeves in this heat. He made a mental note not to mention her appearance again.

"I'm sorry," she said as she slid back into the booth, then stared at him across the table.

Thomas's jaw dropped, and he verbalized his first thought. "You're beautiful." He blinked his eyes a few times and took in her flawless ivory complexion, the way her brown eyes took on a new shine without all that dark makeup, and her gorgeous full lips that he couldn't stop staring at, with only a hint of lipstick.

She covered her face with her hands. "I'm way too over sensitive, and I apologize for getting so upset. I like to think I'm tougher than that."

Thomas reached across the table and eased her hands away from her face. "So that's who has been hiding behind that makeup." He smiled. "Why would you want to hide a face like yours behind all that darkness? You're beautiful," he said again.

Her cheeks blushed as she lowered her head. "Oops. I let my ice cream melt." When she looked back up at him, she smiled. "Will you be staring at me like that from now on?"

"*Ya*, I think I will." He was pretty sure he could look at her constantly for the rest of his life.

"I—I had to wash off my makeup because my mascara ran." She pressed her lips together, then smiled. A real smile.

He gazed across the table. "Don't take this the wrong way, but I sure am glad I made you cry."

She laughed. "Oh, wow. Not sure exactly how I'm supposed to take that, but I guess there's a compliment in there somewhere."

"*Ya*, there is. You're gorgeous." Grinning, he said, "Please don't make me hurt your feelings so you'll cry and go take off your makeup. Maybe just don't wear it anymore." He cringed. He was doing it again. "Sorry. I think that's how I made you cry in the first place. It's just . . . you're so pretty without it."

∼

JANELLE TWISTED her napkin in her lap, relishing the compliments. If he knew everything about her, he wouldn't feel the same way. Beauty didn't run skin deep, but more and more, she wanted to reveal herself to Thomas. She'd first taken an interest in boys when she was about thirteen, but now that she was seventeen—and still never been kissed—guys had taken on a new attraction. She wasn't a kid anymore, but a young woman who longed to be held and loved. And even the most unlikely of scenarios swam through her mind. Janelle was fixated on Thomas's mouth, and he must have noticed because he grinned.

Maybe he would be her first kiss. But that would be as far as it would ever go.

"It's not going to be dark for hours." He nodded to her ice cream, puddled in the bowl. "And unless you're going to drink that, maybe we can go somewhere . . . you know, go do something."

His face turned red, and it was sweet. He was sweet. "Like what?" she asked even though it didn't really matter where they went. She'd go anywhere he suggested.

After he snatched the bill from the table and laid out cash atop it, he put on his hat. "Are you up for about a thirty-minute drive? There's something I'd like to show you. And I'd be happy to pay for your gas to get there."

He was getting sweeter by the moment. "You paid for the ice cream, and I have a full tank of gas." She stood up when he did. "Are you going to tell me where we're going?"

"*Nee*, let it be a surprise." He grinned, then took her hand as they walked out of the café. The Amish were known for not showing affection in public, so Janelle was surprised. It was also the first time a man had held her hand, which only made her long for a more intimate relationship. And that couldn't happen.

She drove down the gravel road heading west for about fifteen minutes until Thomas pointed to their left. "Take that next road."

Janelle did as he said, and after another mile or so, she realized she had never been in this area. "Well, this is a mystery, for sure. I know I haven't lived here long, but

Montgomery isn't all that big, and I've never been down this road."

She glanced to her left, then to her right as she drove. There were Amish farms scattered throughout the area. It was easy enough to tell she was getting deep into an Amish community. No electric poles, there were buggies parked in the driveways, and clothes hung on the line blowing in the wind. Was she taking him to his house?

"Just a little farther, then you'll turn right and go about a mile."

"Here. Turn right here." He pointed to a narrow dirt road that led to a beautiful white farmhouse with a gray porch and white picket fence. Flowers were in full bloom in beds surrounding the house. A wooden porch swing hung between two trees, and an older woman was rocking in it, sipping tea.

"Is it okay to show up unannounced like this?" She instinctively reached for her black sunglasses on the console. "And I thought the Amish didn't like strangers."

He chuckled. "That's kind of harsh, *ya*? Maybe some are stand-offish, but I assure you, we all have non-Amish friends. Not everyone is like Brian and his friends."

"Sorry, but . . ." She slowed the car almost to a stop way before she turned onto the driveway. "What about the way I'm dressed? Normally, I don't care what people think, but if she's a friend of yours . . ."

Thomas gently reached over and eased off her sunglasses. "Trust me, when Fannie gets a look at those brown eyes, flecked with glistening gold and shining an inner light, she won't notice the clothes. And, if she does, so what?"

Oh, how this guy was growing on her. *Danger, danger, danger*. But she just nodded, pulled into the driveway, and the small older woman with gray hair stood from the swing. She was wearing the traditional Amish clothing; a maroon dress, black apron, a prayer covering on her head with gray strands blowing in the breeze, and she was barefoot.

Janelle looked down at her black boots and could recall the feel of the warm summer grass between her toes when she was younger.

Thomas waved as they walked to where the older woman was standing. "*Wie bischt*, Fannie," he said.

"I'm *gut*, Thomas. What brings you here this evening?" She smiled with one tooth missing toward the back. The woman had to be in her eighties, her face a roadmap of lines, but the kindness that shown in her eyes led Janelle to believe it had been a journey well-traveled.

"This is *mei* friend, Janelle."

Janelle had noticed in the car that it was about six-fifteen. "Pleased to meet you, Fannie," she said as she waited for the woman to scan her attire or extend a hand, but sometimes Amish didn't shake hands.

Fannie didn't look her up and down, and she did extend a frail hand. "What a lovely name, Janelle. You're the second Janelle I've met in *mei* life, so I know that it means God is Gracious."

Janelle smiled. "Thank you." Her parents had told her the meaning, and she might not like a lot of things about herself, but her name wasn't on that list. She'd always like her name.

"I bet I know why you're here." Fannie grinned as she scrunched up her face in an almost childlike manner.

"Are they here yet?" Thomas asked, smiling.

"*Ya*, they surely are. Arrived last week." She paused and took a deep breath. "It's a bit of a hike for me in this heat, but you know where to go. And when you get back, I'll have a pitcher of cold tea and plate of blueberry muffins waiting for you."

"*Danki*, Fannie."

And for the second time, Thomas latched on to Janelle's hand.

They left the front yard, rounded the house, and started walking out in an open field.

"Are you going to tell me where we're going?"

"*Nee*." He turned to her and winked, still holding her hand. "But you're going to love it."

CHAPTER 5

Janelle's eyes welled with tears when they reached their destination, and Thomas hoped he hadn't made a mistake. But when she laughed, held her arms high in the air, and spun around in circles, it was confirmation that he had brought her to exactly the right place. Flowers borrowed from every color in the rainbow circled her as the sun rays met with her ivory-colored cheeks, her brown eyes flecked with golden hues. It seemed as if God had created this paradise exclusively for her.

"This is most beautiful . . ." Her voice cracked. "No, I am not going to cry for a second time today, although it wouldn't be for the same reason." She swiped at her eyes as she gazed upon the butterflies, probably more than most people have ever seen in one place. Hundreds, at least.

"The Monarchs arrive here in Indiana usually the last part of June. Fannie plants native flowers that are full of nectar. We see them here in the south before they show up in northern Indiana. When we were *kinner*, we called her the butterfly lady."

Janelle held her arms out to her sides, and it wasn't long before she was covered with butterflies on both sides of her shirt. "They must like black," she said before laughing again. "This is amazing."

Thomas had always heard that butterflies liked bright colors, but he wasn't going to ruin this moment. He stepped back a little, watching her and wishing he had a camera even though they weren't really allowed. Young people in their *rumschpringe* mostly had cell phones, but smartphones were off-limits. No connections to the Internet and no cameras. And if the phones did have a camera, the Amish owner better not get caught using it. Thomas had an ancient flip phone with no camera. Otherwise, he was sure he would have broken the rule.

"It's not the black they like . . . it's you." He motioned with his hands to himself. "Only one little loner thought me worthy, and I've got on black pants and a dark blue shirt." He chuckled, knowing he could watch her like this all day.

Even when she slowly lowered her arms, they circled around her, twinkling in the sunlight, like little fairies of protection.

"Butterflies are spiritual creatures. They're drawn to you for a reason."

She walked toward him, the butterflies following her. "Thank you for bringing me here," she said in a shaky voice. Then she wrapped her arms around him and seemed to hang on for dear life. He would be happy to keep her in his arms for as long as possible.

Janelle had surprised herself with the spontaneous hug, but there truly was something spiritual at play, with the butterflies . . . and with herself. There was a freedom out here in this beautiful field filled with these amazing creatures—and with Thomas whose strong arms pulled her even closer. She was a sweaty mess, but he wasn't much better, though it didn't matter to her and seemingly didn't bother him either.

When they slowly parted, he held her gaze, his eyes on her lips, and she couldn't think of a better place for a first kiss. But she knew not to let that happen, no matter how much she longed for it. At least, not yet. She took an abrupt step back, then spun in a circle.

"Look at them all, Thomas." She danced around, the tall and magnificent flowers almost up to her knees. Even though she'd only known Thomas for a couple of days, she was enjoying her time with him, especially this amazing outing.

"I'd rather just look at you," he said softly, smiling, his eyes intent as he looped his thumbs beneath his suspenders.

Janelle was happy to have a new friend, and no matter how dreamily he looked at her, that was all they could be. Friends. If Thomas Schrock knew everything about her, he'd run away. He was also Amish, and she wasn't—a secondary circumstance that wouldn't ever be up for consideration.

For now, she was going to enjoy the way he was

watching her and pretend she had a different life ahead of her, one filled with love and romance.

After a few more minutes, and with sweat trickling down their faces, they headed back toward Fannie's house.

Janelle kept her hands clasped in front of her since Thomas had held her hand twice already.

∼

THOMAS SETTLED in to one of four white chairs on Fannie's front porch. Janelle slid into another, and after Fannie filled their glasses of ice from a pitcher of tea, she took the seat closest to Janelle. There was a platter full of blueberry muffins on a table in the middle beside three small plates.

"Help yourself to a muffin." Fannie waved an arm over the table, glancing back and forth at Janelle and Thomas, her eyes eventually homing in on Janelle. "What did you think about the butterflies?"

Janelle daintily reached for a muffin. Her face blushed a light pink from the heat as she pushed strands of dark hair away from her face. "They are amazing, so beautiful."

"Did you know that Monarchs migrate back to Indiana every summer, unlike other insects? In the fall, they go to Mexico, then in the summertime, they come back to Indiana to reproduce and lay eggs."

"No, I didn't know that," Janelle said before she took a small bite of her muffin. "This is delicious."

Thomas couldn't take his eyes off her.

Fannie pressed her palms together, grinning. "And the

butterflies you saw today are not the same ones that left in the fall. They are the grandchildren from the butterflies that left us last year."

"They are beautiful, and I've never seen so many in one place." She glanced at Thomas before she turned back to Fannie. "I'm so glad Thomas brought me here, and I appreciate your hospitality."

Fannie smiled. "I enjoy company, and I enjoy sharing the Monarchs." She gently slapped a hand to her leg. "Now tell me all about you. Have you always lived in Montgomery, and we have just never crossed paths?"

"No, ma'am. My family moved here six months ago. My father relocated his construction company here. My mom grew up on a farm in Shoals, and she's always wanted a more small-town feel than where we were living in Indianapolis. Me and my dad were onboard for the move too."

Fannie nodded. "So, you will go back to school when the summer is over? Do you have siblings?" She chuckled. "*Ach*, forgive me if I am asking too many questions. I don't get a lot of visitors."

Thomas took note of the comment, to visit Fannie more.

Janelle waved a dismissive hand with her two black rings on, and her leather bracelet snapped against her tiny wrist. Thomas had known this was a safe place to bring his new friend. Passing judgment was frowned up, but his people could be just as guilty of judgment as some of the English. But Fannie loved everyone.

"No problem at all," Janelle said before she dabbed her mouth with a napkin. "I'm an only child. I'm seventeen, but I finished high school early in Indy. I've been working with my mom at the general store not far from here, mostly part-time, but full-time lately because she's been sick. Nothing serious. I think she'll be back to work tomorrow."

Fannie let out a small gasp. "Is your mother Sharlene Herron, the owner?"

Janelle nodded. "Yes, ma'am."

"*Ach*, I've been in that store many times, and your *mamm* is delightful." Fannie pressed her palms together, smiling again. "We were all so happy when the store opened. It's close and convenient for those of us who don't—or aren't able—to travel far. Will you stay on with her, working there indefinitely?"

Janelle sighed. "I would love that."

Thomas's ears perked up. That was good news to him, too, since he was enjoying getting to know this mysterious girl more than he could have ever anticipated.

"But I won't be able to," Janelle added. "I'll be going off to college when the summer is up." She lowered her head, her lips curling under before she lifted her eyes to Fannie's. "I'm afraid I won't get to enjoy your lovely town for long." She glanced at Thomas, but it wasn't long enough for him to read her expression, and he felt a pang in the pit of his stomach. "I'm scheduled to start at Indiana University. I haven't really decided what I'm going to major in, but I'm leaning toward horticulture."

"These are exciting times for you, then." Fannie raised her tea glass to her lips with shaky hands. After a long sip and brushing back strands of gray hair that had fallen from her prayer covering again, she said, "So, how did you and Thomas meet?"

Thomas locked eyes with Janelle right away, hoping she wouldn't bring up Brian and his friends.

"It's hot outside, and when I saw him walking down the road, I offered him a ride yesterday and today. We just met yesterday." Janelle smiled.

"Thomas is a wonderful boy. I've known him since he was a wee little thing." She tapped a finger to her chin and eyed Thomas. "Although, somewhere along the line, you grew into a man."

He wondered if he was blushing. "*Ya*, I grew up," he said even though he was mentally calculating how much longer Janelle would be in Montgomery before she left for college.

"What made you bring your new friend to see *mei* butterflies?" Fannie used her napkin to dab at sweat on her forehead as she raised an eyebrow, posing the question to Thomas.

He opened his mouth to speak, but he didn't really know what to say. He and Janelle both knew why he brought her here, and he'd seen the joy in her movements and expression. But it was up to her how much she wanted to tell Fannie. He suspected she didn't want to share nearly as much information, the way she had with him, which had been surprising. He barely knew this girl, but there was some sort of connection between them that bypassed just physical attraction.

"Uh . . . I-I um . . ." Janelle took a deep breath.

"Who wouldn't want to see your beautiful butterflies?" Thomas said after Janelle fumbled the words and her face reddened. He probably didn't want her sharing her information anymore than he wanted Fannie to know that she'd picked him up in her car because of bullies.

Fannie nodded. "I agree. Lovely creatures. I look forward to their arrival every year." She sighed, frowning. "I worry who will continue to plant seed or how long the plants will survive after *mei* passing. I'd hate for the Monarchs to stop coming back."

"That would be tragic." Janelle stiffened and shook her head. "We can't let that happen." She smiled at Thomas. "One of us will always make sure the flowers are there to draw the Monarchs back to your beautiful field for generations to enjoy."

"You are a darling *maed* to offer up such kindness to an old lady you just met." She turned to Thomas with her eyebrow raised again.

"*Ya*, we will always make sure that the flowers are kept up so the butterflies will return." Thomas spoke the words, assuming he would be the one to do so. Janelle would be at college. It was confusing why she would make such an offer.

Fannie pointed a finger at Thomas, then at Janelle. "I'm going to hold you to this."

Janelle glanced at Thomas before she smiled and told Fannie, "It's a promise."

Thomas scratched his cheek, pondering her commitment.

CHAPTER 6

Janelle waited until they were in her car before she said, "I'll be home every summer even if it's only for a short visit with my parents." She recognized the confusion on his face when she made the promise. "So, no worries. Even if you're off and married to some Amish woman, I'll make sure the flowers are maintained so the butterflies come back." She offered up a weak smile, pretty sure she wouldn't stay in contact with this sweet Amish guy even though they seemed to have connected to each other quickly.

She reached for her black sunglasses on the console in between them, but Thomas put a hand on hers. "If it's not too bright, leave them off." He grinned. "I like looking at the new you."

When Thomas smiled, her heart rate sped up, and she could feel herself blushing. But she didn't have anything to lose by flirting back. "I will if you take your hat off."

He laughed. "You just want to make fun of *mei* hat hair."

"Exactly." She shrugged, fighting the urge to chuckle as he placed his hat in his lap. Then she rubbed the top of his sweaty hair until it stuck up in all directions, and she couldn't hold back her laughter as she put her hand back on the steering wheel.

He took both hands and did his best effort to finger-comb his hair into submission.

"That's not helping," she said through a smile. He was such a handsome guy. Maybe before she left for college, he would end up being her first kiss after all. Then that would be it, except for maybe an annual visit to the butterfly field.

"So . . ." she said as he pointed for her to turn on the next road. "Like you heard me say earlier, my mom is planning to go back to work tomorrow, but I always bring my own car. I can still drive you the rest of the way to your house since I suspect Brian and those guys will be hanging around." She rolled her eyes. "Or maybe not. They might have moved along and found someone else to pick on."

∼

THOMAS SHOOK HIS HEAD. "*Nee*. I've had a great time with you yesterday and today, but I'm going to have to stand up to those guys." He wasn't looking forward to the smack in the face that was coming, but he disliked Janelle trying to protect him even more.

"Why?" She briefly turned to face him, frowning. "They'll give up eventually." Then she grinned and batted her eyes at him playfully. "Unless you're not being truthful, and you're tired of hanging out with me after work."

He couldn't help but smile as he recalled the moment they'd shared in the butterfly field, a brief few seconds when he'd thought he might kiss her. Until she broke the moment and stepped away. *What was that about anyway?* A first kiss was special, so it either wasn't the right time, or he wasn't the right man.

"*Nee*, that's not it." He ran a hand through his hair again, still damp from the heat. He shrugged. "I'm not going to have a girl keep protecting me."

"I'm seventeen. I'm a woman, not a girl." She cut her eyes at him with one corner of her mouth turned up in a half-smile. "And that's a bit chauvinistic, don't you think?"

Thomas had only been schooled through the eighth grade like all the Amish in his community. He hadn't heard the word chauvinistic before, but he thought he understood what she was saying. "I can take care of myself."

She turned onto the road to his house. "I'm not saying that you can't, but I know it goes against what you believe." She lifted her right arm, the one with her black leather bracelet. "Remember, I have my own reminder that violence isn't the answer. Just avoid those bullies and stay away from them."

"*Ya*, maybe." If he held firm to his decision, he might not get to spend any more time with her.

She pulled into his driveway and twisted to face him. "See you tomorrow?"

He rubbed his chin. "Under one condition."

After sighing heavily, she asked, "What condition?"

"That you don't wear any makeup. You're so pretty, and you shouldn't cover up your face." He held up a hand when she opened her mouth to speak. "And I do understand about the caterpillar/butterfly thing. Let it be a sign that you trust me, even if just a little, and want to get to know me better." He grinned. "Because I'm enjoying getting to know you."

She stared at him, chewing on her lip. "Okay," she finally said.

Thomas opened the car door. "Then I'll see you tomorrow."

Janelle nodded, then pulled away slowly as she eyed the farmhouse Thomas lived in with his family. White exterior, gray porch, like Fannie's house, although Thomas's house was more pristine with even more blooming flowers in the beds, freshly mowed grass, and what appeared to be a fresh coat of paint on the white picket fence.

As she drove away, she wondered what it was like to live such a simple life. There had to be some freedom in not having to compete with each other, along with other disciplines that kept life simple. But as sweat from her black shirt stuck to the back of her car seat, even with the air conditioning blowing on high, she couldn't imagine how hot it must get inside their houses.

After pondering the Amish lifestyle and recalling her time with the butterflies, she was finally home and went straight to her mother's bedroom, panicked when her mom wasn't there. After crossing through the living room, she found her in the kitchen, up and dressed.

"Welcome home," her mother said with her head

lowered as she appeared to be searching for something in the refrigerator. She straightened, holding a bottle of ketchup, then gasped. "Your face!"

Instinctively, Janelle reached up and cupped her cheeks. "What's wrong?"

Her mom closed the space between them and pulled her into a hug, kissing her on the cheek. "I just don't get to see your beautiful face often enough." She eased her away, keeping a hold on her arms and smiling.

"Mom, you see my face every night after I shower and wash off my makeup." She rolled her eyes before sighing, then took a seat at the kitchen table.

"Did you take the Amish man home? Is he the reason you let him see you without all the makeup?" Her mother pulled out a kitchen chair and sat across the table from her.

Janelle avoided her mother's inquisitive eyes. "Maybe."

"He's Amish. And, you know that—"

Janelle groaned. "We've had this conversation, Mom. I just met the guy yesterday. He's super nice, and it would be great to have a friend for the next month before I leave for school. Trust me . . . I don't have any romantic illusions." She paused. "Nor will I ever."

"Baby girl, I love you. And one day you will find the perfect person for you." Her mother stood and extended a hand to Janelle's elbow. "You are beautiful, inside, and out. And don't you forget it." She got up with the bottle of ketchup in her hand and moved to the counter. "Meatloaf sound okay?"

"Yep. Sounds great. I'm glad to see you're out of bed and seem better."

With her back to Janelle, her mom began adding ingredients to meat she already had in a bowl. "I feel good. Not a hundred percent, but well enough to go back to the store tomorrow. So, if you want to take a day off tomorrow—"

"No, I'll go in."

Her mother peered at her over her shoulder and grinned. "Okay."

"And not just because of Thomas, Mom. I like working there." Janelle was overly friendly to every customer who came into the shop, not wanting her mother to lose any sales because of the way Janelle dressed. And her kindness had always been returned.

She lifted herself from the chair. "But I'm going to go upstairs unless you need help in here."

"Nope. I'm good, Honey."

Janelle trudged up the stairs. If she had a nickel every time her parents told her she was beautiful inside and out, she'd be wealthy woman.

She closed her bedroom door, locked it, and then went to her full-length mirror and stared at herself, recalling a time when she really was kind of pretty on the outside. But as she peeled off her black shirt and stared at herself wearing only a white lacy bra that no husband would ever see, she closed her eyes, and prayed that when she opened them, a different reflection would stare back at her. The same thing she'd done for the past three years since the fire.

But she was still scarred from her chest all the way to her feet. Despite numerous and painful skin grafts, her lumpy discolored skin was a constant reminder of her carelessness. For reasons she'd never understand, God had spared her face and lower arms. But what man would ever want to take her in his arms, be physically close to her, and feel what her heart had to offer when her body was so repulsive?

∾

THE NEXT DAY, Thomas was surprised to see that Brian and his friends weren't loitering anywhere in sight. He also didn't see Janelle outside the store, so he trekked in that direction. There were two cars in the parking lot. She said her mother would be back at work today, or maybe it was a customer.

He latched on to the handrail, not a necessity, but it helped with the metal pin in his leg, then ascended the three steps to the country store entry door. He could remember the Lantzs owning the small house and living in it before Janelle's family purchased it, knocked out most of the walls, and turned it into a general store/gift shop.

A bell jingled on the door when he pushed it open, and a blast of cool air welcomed him into the space that smelled like cinnamon. He'd been in the store once to pick up a few things his mother needed, but he doubted Janelle's mother would remember him, assuming it was her car parked outside.

His brown work boots echoed against the wood floor even though he tried to step lightly.

Janelle's mother came from around the corner of a huge shelf that had various cooking utensils on pegs.

"Hello," she said as she approached him. "Can I help you find something?"

The woman was older, but he could see where Janelle got her beautiful features.

"Uh, *ya* . . . I'm looking for Janelle." He took off his hat when the woman extended her hand.

"I'm going to take a wild guess that you might be Thomas?" She smiled before she let go of his hand.

He felt his face turning red, flattered that Janelle had told her mother about him. "*Ya*, yes, ma'am. Nice to meet you."

"The pleasure is mine." She held up a finger. "Wait right here." She waved her hand in a circle. "Or have a look around. Janelle is in the back office doing some accounting work for me. I'll go get her."

Thomas nodded but didn't move. He tapped his hat against the side of his leg and swallowed hard. What if those guys had been out there? He would have been smacked for sure.

"Oh no!" Janelle came running toward him. "I'm so sorry. I completely lost track of time. Were Brian and—"

"*Nee*, they weren't there." He smiled, happy to see she wasn't wearing any makeup.

She clapped her hands a couple of times and bounced up on her toes. "See. I told you they would get bored."

He nodded over his shoulder. "Um . . . I guess I can walk the rest of the way home since it sounds like you're busy."

She put her hands on her hips, frowning. Her long dark hair flowed to her waist, and she was wearing a black long-sleeved shirt and pants as usual. Thomas wondered how many black clothes she owned. The blouses and pants were always different, but always black.

"I thought we were going to hang out," she said, leaning her weight to one side, her lip rolled into an exaggerated pout. "But I get it if you've made other plans." She raised an eyebrow as she lifted her chin.

Thomas chuckled. "*Nee*, I didn't make any other plans."

"Great. I'll be right back."

She returned less than a minute later toting a black purse as her mother followed behind her. "Bye, Mom," she said over her shoulder.

Her mother waved. "Have fun, and it was nice to meet you, Thomas."

He put on his hat. "Nice to meet you too."

After they were in Janelle's car and she'd started the engine, she turned toward him. "Where to?"

He rubbed his chin. "I was thinking about places I could show you that maybe you hadn't seen. And there's an old rundown farm outside of town. No one has lived there for years, but it has a great pond, and there used to be a picnic table near the water." He paused, considering the way she was dressed. "There's a giant tree for shade, but it'll still be hot. We can go somewhere else if you want to, somewhere with air conditioning."

She shook her head. "Nope. I love being by the water, any kind of water . . . the beach, the ocean, a creek, or even a pond." She put the car in park. "Wait here. I'm going to go back inside and get us some drinks and snacks to take."

Janelle was out of the car and jogging toward the store

before Thomas had time to say anything. She returned with a picnic basket a few minutes later.

"Check it out," she said as she stowed the basket in the backseat, slammed the door, then hopped in up front. "My mom said for us to use this. It still has the price tag on it, but it has a compartment to keep things cold. I put in some ready-made sandwiches, chips, drinks . . ." She shrugged. "In case we stay there long enough to work up an appetite, it could be dinner."

Thomas's people referred to the evening meal as supper, but he didn't care how it was defined. He was thrilled she wanted to spend that much time with him.

"Hey, before we leave, do you want to grab a swimsuit? I have shorts on under *mei* pants." He smiled. "I was hoping you would want to go to the pond, and it would be a *gut* way to cool off."

His smile faded when he looked at her. Her face was ashen as her bottom lip trembled.

"I don't swim," she said before she put the car in drive.

"Are you sure you don't want to grab something to at least be able to dangle your feet in the water?" He briefly eyed her long black pants, tight around her ankles and her black boots. He raised his palms and grinned, hoping to shift her expression. "I promise I have no ulterior motives." Then he recalled her caterpillar/butterfly metamorphosis. She wasn't ready to trust him that much. "I just thought if it got too hot, we might get in the water. It's not deep. At least, it wasn't the last time I was there. I promise not to let you drown if we take a dip."

"I don't swim," she repeated between gritted teeth.

He shrugged. "That's fine. We've got food and drinks. It'll be fun. Turn right."

She made the turn, but her face was stone cold before she put on her dark sunglasses and kept her eyes on the road.

CHAPTER 7

Janelle regretted the harsh way she'd spoken to Thomas. It was a quiet ride to the old farmhouse, and when they turned onto a weedy dirt road, she saw the pond in the distance.

She followed the road as far as it would go.

"We'll have to walk the rest of the way," he said. After she put the car in park, he reached over and touched her arm. "I'm sorry. Going swimming isn't a big deal. When you said you liked any kind of water, ocean, etc. . . . it was just a thought."

She lowered her head. "No, I'm the one who should be sorry. I shouldn't have snapped at you that way."

He was probably waiting for an explanation, but she opened the car door, then retrieved the basket from the backseat. Thomas walked around the car and eased it from her hand. "I'll carry this. You watch for snakes."

She let out a nervous chuckle. "You're kidding, right?"

He shrugged. "You never know."

Janelle jerked the basket out of his hand. "I'll carry this.

You watch for snakes." Then she latched on to his one of his suspenders with her free hand. "Lead the way. I'll just step where you step."

He laughed, and so did she. They were back on comfortable ground. Ground that hopefully wouldn't reveal a snake in their path.

"It's still here," Thomas said when they reached the picnic table.

After a snake-free hike in the heat through a field, Janelle let go of his suspenders, brushed crispy leaves from the worn tabletop, and set the basket down. A huge oak tree and the cool breeze made the heat tolerable. Janelle recalled a time when she would have worn shorts and a sleeveless top.

She took in her surroundings . . . the old farmhouse with peeling white paint, a porch missing several boards, and an unpainted barn that was leaning to one side. "Who used to live here? I always wonder how property ends up in this condition." She tried to picture it with a coat of fresh paint, white picket fence, and flowerbeds filled with colorful flowers. "It's sad."

"An older Amish couple lived there. I heard their kids left and were never baptized into the faith. But it seems like they would have sold the property or fixed up the place. I guess we are kind of trespassing, but lots of people come here to fish or swim, and I've never heard of anyone getting in trouble. It's not even fenced so there are lots of ways to get onto the property." He shrugged. "Look." Thomas pointed to the pond, like a small twinkling ocean with tiny waves from the gentle breeze.

Janelle sat on top of the table, and Thomas sat beside

her. "It is really pretty." She turned to him. "Would you have really swam in that pond? I mean, you can if you want to. But aren't there snakes in there?"

He chuckled. "You're a city girl. We grew up swimming in ponds like this. The snakes are more afraid of us than we are of them. Seen plenty, but they never bothered us."

She shivered. "Snakes terrify me."

"Well . . ." he gazed into her eyes. "You're safe with me."

She tipped her head to one side and locked eyes with him. "And why is that? I mean, why do I feel safe with you?"

He shrugged. "Because I'm a great guy I guess."

She nudged him with her shoulder. "With a big ego. But yeah . . . you do seem like a great guy." She twisted around to where the picnic basket was and pulled out two cold bottles of water and handed him one. "You know, I'll only be here for a few weeks before I leave for school."

"*Ya*, I figured." He lowered his head.

"But you seem to know all these secret little spots, and I'd love to spend the next few weeks doing things with you if you have time, you know . . . like after work or on the weekends. But if you're busy—"

"I have some vacation time coming. Maybe I could take off some time and show you around properly, all these secret little spots as you called them."

"Wow. That would be awesome."

"And I have some news." He winked at her, which made her heart flutter.

When he was quiet, she chuckled. "Are you going to tell me, or do I need to guess?"

He smiled. "I have a new horse, and *mei* buggy will be ready tomorrow. As much as I like the air conditioning in your car, how would you feel about traveling around with me in *mei* repaired buggy?"

She pressed her hands together as she let out a small gasp. "I would love that. I've never ridden in an Amish buggy."

He scrunched up his face. "Really?"

"Remember, I haven't been here that long. I didn't go to school here. Most of the people I've met have been when I was working at the store, and repno offense, but most Amish girls my age don't seem interested in being friends with someone who dresses the way I do. And I've been fine with that." She paused. "At least I thought I was." She locked eyes with him. "But I'm enjoying spending time with you." She looked away when she felt a blush coming on. "It's nice to have a new friend."

∾

THOMAS WANTED to be a lot more than friends with Janelle, but the odds of that happening were not stacked in his favor. She wasn't Amish, and she would be leaving at the end of the summer. He made a mental point to care for her, but he couldn't fall in love with her. He wasn't even sure if people could fall in love in a few weeks. Either way, he already felt weird about her leaving.

"Do you believe in fate?" she asked as she handed him a sandwich.

He shook his head. "*Nee*, not really. I believe *Gott* gives us free will to make choices."

"I believe that, too, but if I hadn't looked out the window at just the right time, I wouldn't have seen those guys giving you a hard time. We probably wouldn't have ever met."

He swallowed his bite of sandwich, took a sip of water. "True. But you made the choice to come . . ." He rolled his eyes. ". . . to come save me."

She grinned. "Yeah, I did."

They were quiet for a while after they ate. Thomas draped his arm around her shoulder, and she startled, so he drew it back. "Sorry."

She took his arm, put it back around her, held his hand, and said, "Don't be. It just caught me off guard." Then she laid her head on his shoulder.

Thomas had put his arm around girls before, even kissed a few, but he'd never felt the way he did right now, as if his heart might explode. He breathed in the aroma of her dark hair that smelled like lavender. "Is this your true hair color?" he finally asked.

She looked up at him, close enough that he could have kissed her, and he wanted to, but he held his position, truly wanting to know.

"Yep," she finally said. "It's the only thing about me that's real. In every other way, I'm still that caterpillar, learning who I am. But God gave me this dark-colored hair."

Thomas took his free hand and tucked a few loose strands behind her ear. "It's beautiful." He gazed into her eyes.

"You want to kiss me, don't you?" She bit her bottom lip. "I told you I've never been kissed."

He hung his head. "*Ya*, I know. And a first kiss should be something special." He glanced at her. "Probably not when we're a sweaty mess and sitting on a picnic table."

They both turned when they heard rustling weeds. "Oh no," Janelle said as Thomas took his arm from around her.

"I thought I recognized your car from the main road, Goth girl." Brian walked up to them and chuckled. "Wow, you're halfway decent-looking without all that dark makeup." He turned his attention to Thomas and folded his arms across his chest. "And exactly what are you two doing out here?" He nodded to Janelle. "Trying to get a little action? I guess even Amish guys want a good piece of—"

"Shut up, Brian." Thomas stood up, his blood boiling as his heart pounded against his chest like a bass drum. "Just leave us alone." He balled his fists at his sides as Brian edged closer to Janelle, who took a step backward.

Brian held up a hand. "Calm down. I'm not here to give you any grief." He eyed the picnic basket. "Although I am a little hungry."

"There's nothing left." Janelle folded her arms across her chest. "Are you like stalking us or something? What's the point in that anyway?"

Brian walked closer to her, but Janelle held her ground this time and didn't back up. "Don't flatter yourself." He studied her face for far too long. "Although I meant what I said. You're kind of pretty without all that makeup." He touched her arm. "What cha hiding underneath all that black clothing?"

Janelle stepped backward, her lip trembling.

"Don't touch her," Thomas said as he rushed to Janelle and stood in front of her. "If your *daed* has a beef with mine because we offer fairer prices on construction jobs, then maybe your *daed* needs to lower his prices and be more competitive. And not send his son to bully people."

"What did you call me?" Brian squinted his eyes at Thomas as he puffed out his chest and squared his shoulders.

"Let's just go," Janelle said as she tugged on Thomas's sleeve.

"Yeah, just go, Thomas." He could tell by the look in Brian's eyes that the guy would have no qualms about punching him square in the jaw. "After you apologize for calling me a bully," Brian added.

"*Nee*, you are a bully. I won't apologize for that." Thomas braced himself for what was coming.

Brian nodded. "Well, okay, then . . ." He shoved Thomas out of the way and latched on to one of Janelle's arms hard enough that she yelped.

"Let go of her." Thomas grabbed Brian's arm and slung it away from Janelle, then Brian's punch in his face knocked him to his knees, the taste of blood from his nose trickling into his mouth.

Janelle was quickly by his side, crying, and yelling for Brian to leave. But when Brian yanked Janelle to her feet and began to drag her away, she kicked and screamed. "We're gonna have a look at what's underneath your Goth clothes," he said between gritted teeth.

A force stronger than Thomas's faith catapulted him to his feet, and he ran toward Brian and shoved him down. Unfortunately, Janelle fell, too, but scrambled to her feet and got out of the way. "Stop!" she screamed when she saw Brian ball up his hand.

Thomas ducked when Brian's fist came flying toward him, and then he punched Brian with all the bottled anger he'd been holding onto.

Brian stumbled backward, shouted some foul words, then charged at Thomas.

But Thomas hit him and hit him again . . . and again. Until Brian turned and limped away.

"Hey!" Thomas yelled as he walked to where Brian had slowly stopped and swiveled around. He needed to see exactly how badly he had hurt the guy. Not any more than Brian had hurt him, he supposed. Brian's first blow had been spot-on. Thomas swallowed back tears building in his throat, partly from the pain coming from his nose and above his eye, but he also couldn't believe he had inflicted this type of bodily harm on another human being. It tore at his insides. But when Brian had threatened Janelle, he'd lost his ability to remain passive, something that had been drilled into his head for as long as he could remember.

He waited for Brian to swing at him, deciding he wouldn't hit him again. He'd just take it as punishment for his retaliation.

Brian grinned. "I didn't think you had it in you."

Thomas faced off with him. "Now you know," he said.

Janelle rushed into Thomas's arms and buried her chest against his blood-soaked blue shirt as Brian walked away. "We need to get you to the hospital," she said after Brian had stumbled back toward the road and sped away.

Thomas pulled her closer and just held her.

CHAPTER 8

"Are you sure you don't want to go to the hospital?" Janelle's mother asked Thomas from where he sat at the kitchen table, her mother's entire stock of first aid items spread out in front of them.

Janelle sat beside him holding his hand under the table as her mother gently wiped blood from Thomas's face with a wet rag. Thomas had refused to go to the hospital. *People will talk*, he'd said. And he didn't want to go home and have his family see him covered in blood.

Janelle's father paced the kitchen, letting out an occasional sigh as he shook his head. "Brian Edwards is just like his father. We've lived here long enough for me to know that much."

"I shouldn't have hit him, but when he went after Janelle . . ." He flinched when Janelle's mother dabbed the rag on his cut lip.

"Son, I'm well aware that the Amish are passive, and it tears me up that Brian put you in a position to go against your beliefs." He stopped pacing and ran a hand through his salt and pepper hair. "But when I think about what could have happened to our daughter if you hadn't intervened, it makes me want to go find the guy and beat the snot out of him."

"I think there's been enough fighting today," Janelle's mother said as she applied ointment on the cut above Thomas's right eye.

"*Mei* family will be disappointed in me." Thomas felt shame wrapping around him like a serpent squeezing the life out of him.

"I am happy to take you home and explain to your family that you were protecting our daughter." Janelle's father sat across from Thomas. "They will understand."

Thomas knew better. "*Danki*—I mean, thank you—sir, but that won't be necessary."

Janelle squeezed his hand again. "I'm so sorry you were put in that position."

Her mother began putting all her supplies back in the first aid box. "It's not as bad as it looked at first. You don't need any stitches, but you'll be sore for a while, and you might have a black eye in a day or two."

"*Danki*, ma'am." Thomas cringed when he reached up and touched the bandage above his eye.

"Sharlene," she said. "Please just call me Sharlene." She nodded to Janelle's father who had begun to pace again. "And that is Roger, Janelle's father, obviously."

Thomas shook Janelle's father's hand when he offered it to him. "We owe you a huge amount of gratitude, son."

"*Nee*, you don't. I would do it again if anyone tried to hurt Janelle."

Thomas watched Janelle's parents exchange glances,

slight smiles on their faces that seemed to be mixed with sympathy. They knew, as Janelle did, that Thomas had done something his people were forbidden to do.

"Excuse me." Janelle let go of his hand abruptly, stood, and left the room. "I'll be right back."

∼

THOMAS WATCHED Janelle walk away as his insides churned. He tried to picture the looks on his parents' faces—and his sisters' expressions—when they saw that he had been in a fight. Their disappointment in him would amplify his shame, and even though God frowned upon shame, Thomas couldn't shed the emotion.

Roger sat down at the far end of the table across from Sharlene and was randomly running his hand through his dark hair, specked with gray. Janelle had obviously inherited her dark hair from her father, both in deep contrast to Janelle's mother's blonde hair.

Thomas had a headache, unsure how much of it was because of the fight or how much of his pain was caused by his fear to face his family.

Janelle's father opened his mouth to say something, but instead, his eyes rounded, and he smiled.

Thomas looked over his shoulder when he heard footsteps. And what he saw put a big smile on his face as he eyed the beautiful woman entering the kitchen. His new friend was wearing blue jeans, not black pants. She had on a light blue long-sleeved shirt buttoned almost to her neck along with white socks and blue tennis shoes. His caterpillar shined like a butterfly even though her face was beet red.

Sharlene stood, tearfully walked to her daughter, and kissed her on the forehead. "You look beautiful."

Janelle lowered her head and mumbled, "Thanks."

Thomas stared at her and forced himself not to stand up and shout out the words her mother had just spoken.

"Come on, Roger. Let these two have some time alone." Sharlene motioned for her husband to follow her.

Janelle's father did as she requested, but he paused when he got to his daughter, then drew her into a big hug, kissing the top of her head.

This moment was significant. Thomas was sure of it. Her parents felt the weight of this transformation probably much more than he did.

After her parents' footsteps had faded and they were out of earshot, Thomas stood and faced the beautiful woman in front of him. He wanted to pull her into his arms and kiss her with all the passion he felt, but he reminded himself that she'd never been kissed. He swallowed hard. "Wow," was all he managed to say in a whisper.

Janelle was still blushing as she bit her bottom lip. "It's the least I can do after the sacrifice you made for me."

"Why now?" He was pretty sure he knew there was more to it than thanking him for defending her, but he wanted to hear her say it. "The real reason," he added as his eyes stayed locked with hers.

She took her time before she answered. "You know why."

Thomas took a step closer to her, and again, he tucked

her dark hair behind her ears, lingering, but reminded himself this wasn't the time to kiss her. "Tell me."

Smiling slightly, she said, "I like you. I want to get to know you better. And . . . I trust you because there is something about you that seems to understand me. And that has nothing to do with the fight." She cringed. "Although I hate that happened."

Thomas struggled not to flinch when she gently cupped one side of his face, the side that wasn't as banged up or bandaged but still tender to her gentle touch. "I'm okay," he whispered.

"You're more than okay in my eyes." She leaned up and as her lips brushed his cheek, the urge to take her in his arms was about to overpower him. "But I better take you home. You're going to have to face your family at some point."

Thomas's awareness of his situation returned, slapping him back to reality. "*Ya*, I know."

IT WAS an hour later when Janelle pulled onto the gravel road that led to Thomas's house. "You're going to have to stop staring at me, or I'm going back to my black clothes." His adoring eyes had stayed focused on her since she'd walked into the kitchen at her house. She'd never wanted anyone to kiss her as much as she did now, to feel Thomas's lips on hers, but she wondered how he would feel if he saw the ugliness beneath her new attire. He wouldn't look at her this way again.

"I have to work tomorrow, but I can take some time

off, like I said, and show you around some more." He reached for her hand and squeezed it. "You look truly beautiful."

Janelle felt herself blushing. "*Danki.*" She grinned. "See, I've learned a few Amish words since I've been here."

He let go of her hand. "I guess I better go face the music, as they say."

"Do you want me to come in with you?" She was sure he didn't, but she wanted him to know she was willing to stand by his side when he faced his family.

He shook his head. "*Nee.* It might be ugly, and that's not how I want you to meet *mei* family." He opened the car door and stepped out, then leaned down from where he stood. "Still want to go riding around in *mei* buggy? I'll pick it up after work tomorrow, so I won't be able to stop by the store. It'll be too late. But maybe the next day?"

Janelle nodded. "I'd love that."

He winked at her, then closed the door and trudged to his house like a man about to walk a plank on a ship. Janelle's heart hurt for him, and she said a quick prayer before she gave a final wave as he looked over his shoulder, then entered the house.

∽

Janelle's parents were sitting on the couch in the living room when she got home, neither reading nor watching television. What had they talked about while she'd been gone?

"What's up?" she asked as she sat in the recliner across from them.

Her parents exchanged glances, neither one of them smiling.

"Um, first of all . . . as I told you before, you look beautiful. I hope this new look is one you will be keeping." Her mother cleared her throat. "Your clothes choices are your own, but we know there is meaning attached to your actions, and . . ."

"What your mother is trying to say is, we don't want to see you get hurt. We see the way you look at that boy. You're leaving for school in a few weeks, and summer romances can be tricky, especially this one since Thomas is Amish."

"And . . ." Her mother smiled. "I saw the way he looks at you too."

They were right, but Janelle rolled her eyes anyway. "We barely know each other, and there is nothing romantic going on." That might not be entirely true since they'd held hands, she'd kissed him on the cheek, and he'd gone against everything he believed to protect her. Did those displays of affection lean toward romance? It didn't matter, she supposed. By the end of the summer, she would probably have a broken heart. Even if she wasn't going off to school, she would have ended it. She wanted to remember the way Thomas looks at her now, not what his expression would be if he saw scars covering most of her body. She would never let that happen and had come to terms with a life without a partner.

Her parents exchanged concerned looks again. "Enjoy your time together, just be careful," her mother said.

"Wow. All this worry." She frowned. "I thought you'd be glad I was shedding my skin, so to speak, although that applies to snakes too." Her parents looked confused, but Janelle fondly recalled her time with Thomas, prior to the fight, as she'd held his suspenders, him leading the way and watching for snakes.

"We understand that you need to do things at your own pace, and making this drastic change seems to indicate you might have feelings for Thomas." Her mother held up a hand when Janelle opened her mouth to speak. "We trust your judgment, but we wouldn't be good parents if we didn't voice our concerns. That's all." Her mother gave a slight shrug. "We love you."

Janelle was blessed with awesome parents. She knew she shouldn't take that for granted. "I love you guys too."

Janelle excused herself and went to her bedroom before she began to cry. She glanced at the red suitcase her mother had placed in her room so she could pack for school. She'd never wanted to go to college, but her father had said it would be a waste of a brilliant mind since her grades had always been so good and she'd graduated from high school early. She'd taken lots of online college classes because horticulture interested her. She just wasn't thrilled about being in a school environment.

Following her thoughts about leaving for school, she let her mind drift to a place she didn't often allow, the dreamy place in her mind where she looked normal from head to toe, where she ran her mother's store and lived in this quaint town . . . and even had a husband. Someone like Thomas. That was not the hand she'd been dealt.

CHAPTER 9

Thomas walked into the empty living room. He was late for supper, and he could hear forks clanking against plates in the dining room, so he shuffled into the room with a knot in the pit of his stomach. He'd cleaned up and wiped the blood from his clothes as best he could when he was at Janelle's house, but he still looked a mess in addition to the bandage above his eye.

His mother was the first one to gasp, followed by similar reactions from his sisters.

"You were in another accident, weren't you? Was the *Englisch maed* driving? Was she hurt too?" She pushed her chair back and walked to where he was standing, closely eying the bandage above his eye, his busted lip, and his swollen skin.

He shifted his eyes toward his father who was scowling. "You were in a fight, weren't you?"

Maybe it was the nature of his wounds that led his father to the truth. Thomas nodded, unsure whether he would be eating any supper tonight. It appeared his family was almost finished with the meal, and by the time his father got through with him, he doubted he would have an appetite.

His mother put a hand to her chest and found her way back to her seat at the table. "Thomas, what happened? Fighting is not our way." She blinked back tears, which broke Thomas's heart. He knew it would be like this. "We deserve an explanation."

He gave them a quick summation of what had happened.

His mother and sisters lowered their heads, as if sympathetic for him . . . and Janelle. He waited for his mother to say she forgave him under the circumstances that he had been presented with, but she stayed quiet. His sisters knew better than to get involved and stayed silent.

When his mother didn't say anything, his father straightened in his chair and cut his eyes in Thomas's direction. "You know what the *Ordnung* says about this. We don't use violence no matter—"

"Then what should I have done, *Daed*?" Thomas surprised himself by letting his anger rise to the surface. "Let Brian haul her off into the woods and hurt her? Because I believe that is what would have happened." He'd never bucked up to his father before and seeing his father's face turn beat red as he stood made Thomas quake in his boots. He'd had plenty of spankings when he was little, which in hindsight, seemed a little contradictory to the conversation they were having.

"The Lord intervenes when He is able. We are not to pass judgment, even on someone like the Edwards boy.

Our Amish beliefs span decades of avoiding this type of behavior, and it can't be tolerated."

"*Ach*, well, then maybe I don't need to be baptized into the Amish faith because I would do it all over again." It was true, but didn't his father realize how much his own actions tormented him? Where was even an ounce of compassion for what could have happened to Janelle? He turned to his mother when he heard sniffling, knowing it was every parent's fear that their child would choose to leave, to not be baptized into the faith. Thomas had never considering leaving. Until now.

His father pointed past the living room. "We will take this conversation outside."

Thomas walked briskly ahead of his father, passed through the living room, then sat in a rocking chair on the porch. His headache was back, his eye throbbed, and his lip had started to bleed again.

His father handed him a handkerchief before he sat in a rocking chair next to Thomas, and he used it to dab at his lip. The sun had begun to make its descent, but it was a long time until nightfall this time of year. Thomas wondered how long his father would want to talk. What type of punishment was he considering? His father was the head of the household, and Thomas still lived under his roof. He would accept whatever penance he had coming.

In his heart, he knew what he had done was wrong, but he also believed he didn't have a choice, and he questioned why God had put him in that situation. Was it a test? One that he'd failed. Would Janelle have freed herself and defended herself if Thomas hadn't intervened? Was

Thomas's involvement necessary? He was questioning everything now, even his own place in the Amish community. His father was quiet, likely considering an ample punishment.

"I was in a fight once." His father turned to Thomas. "And I looked a lot worse than you do now. Did you at least get the better of Brian Edwards?"

Thomas's jaw dropped. He was too stunned to speak at first. "You were in a fight?" *Then why did you just rip me to pieces inside?*

His father raised a bushy dark eyebrow. "Well? How did Brian look?"

"Uh . . ." He was still confused as he dabbed his lip with his father's handkerchief again. "I guess he looked worse than me."

His father nodded. Thomas waited for an explanation. When none came, he said, "Who did you get in a fight with?"

Benjamin Schrock rarely cracked a smile, and under the circumstances, Thomas was even more confused. "Brian's father," he said as he scratched his cheek. "Probably when I was about your age." His father pointed a finger at him. "Your *mamm* doesn't know, and I'd like to keep it that way. I was hard on you in there because what you did was wrong. But . . ." He shook his head. "I understand because the men in that family are bullies. What I did was wrong, also, but Brian's father pushed me to my breaking point too. It didn't have anything to do with your *mudder*, but he threatened a friend of mine with a baseball bat, and I'm pretty sure he was going to beat the daylights out of him, so I snatched the bat from him and tossed it in the woods. He jumped me right away. I chose to defend myself."

Thomas didn't know what to say.

His father stood, stared out at the sky, and squinted before he looked at Thomas and grinned again. "He was left looking worse than me, but *mei daed* lined me out with a list of chores for the next month."

Here it comes. The punishment. Thomas held his breath.

"You're spending a lot of time with the *Englisch maed, ya?*" His father frowned. "It won't work, any type of romance you are heading into. It rarely does."

"We're just friends. She's leaving for college in a few weeks." Just saying the words caused his stomach to churn, and he couldn't look at his father for fear that his father would pick up on the torment he was already feeling.

His father ran his hand the length of his beard. "*Ach*, well . . . I reckon that will be punishment enough." Then he walked inside.

Thomas stayed on the porch. His head throbbed, his face felt like it was swelling even more, but it was his heart that hurt the most. He had let himself fall for an English girl. His father must have picked up on that somehow. But his parents didn't have anything to worry about.

Janelle would be gone in a few weeks.

CHAPTER 10

"This is so cool." Janelle had pulled her hair into a ponytail, worn blue jeans again, and had chosen a long-sleeved pink shirt that was thick enough that no one could see her scars beneath the light coloring. She smiled at Thomas who was on the driver's side of the bench in his good-as-new buggy. And his mare was a beautiful mixture of brown and white. "I will remember this for the rest of my life, riding in a buggy for the first time."

Thomas chuckled. "Trust me, the newness wears off, especially when August gets here, and it's unbearably hot."

"Why don't you have one of those buggies I see sometimes that don't have a top?"

He glanced her way as he held onto the reins, keeping the horse in a fast trot. "We call those spring buggies. And believe it or not, it's worse to have the sun bearing down on you, not to mention a sunburn on a sunny day."

She giggled. "I bet it was a nice break for you, riding in my car for a while."

"*Ya*, it was."

They were on their way to see a Bald Eagle nest today, and Thomas had told her a list of places he wanted to take her. He'd taken vacation, a few days here, and a few days there, to spend time with her before she left for school, which left her with a sinking feeling every time she thought about leaving. But until then, they still had plans to see a hidden cave Thomas knew about on one of their trips, take a picnic lunch to a new place this time, and a host of other activities, ending with another trip to see the Monarchs.

Janelle's mother had told her to take as much time away from the store as she wanted.

She turned to Thomas and stared at his eye that had turned a little black over the past couple days, but the swelling had gone down. He still had a bandage above his eye, but his lip was healed. At least, it appeared to be. Janelle wanted him to be her first kiss. It would be a painful goodbye kiss, but she was sure she wanted it to be with Thomas.

"We're going to have a *gut* time." He paused and kept his eyes looking forward. "For as long as you're here."

She heard regret in his voice and considered telling him she would be home for the holidays, but what was the point in seeing him again? Her feelings were already growing for him, and she sensed he felt the same way. One goodbye would be enough. Why drag it out with continual visits and goodbyes every time she visited her parents?

"How long will the Monarchs be in the area?" Maybe

she could at least sneak over to Fannie's when she came home for a first visit if they were still around.

"They leave in the fall. The time varies, but they seem to stay at Fannie's place for longer than anywhere else." He shrugged. "I guess because of all those native flowers in one place."

She recalled the promise she'd made to always come back in the summer to tend to the plants if something happened to Fannie. Janelle would keep her promise. The Amish married younger than non-Amish people, and she wondered if Thomas would have a wife by next June or July when the butterflies returned. Hopefully, Fannie would be around for many more years, but Janelle guessed the woman to be in her mid to late eighties.

"Is it okay if I write to you at school?" He winked at her. "It'll be fun to hear about life in the city."

"Sure." Janelle wouldn't write him back. It would be easier that way. She pushed her dark sunglasses up on her head when the sun went behind the clouds. "Have you ever wanted to leave here? I mean, not be Amish and have all the modern conveniences you live without?"

"Sometimes, I have a random thought about it." He chuckled. "Usually when I'm mad at *mei* parents or *mei* sisters are annoying me, but then I remind myself that I won't always live there."

"You might even be married by this time next year." She heard the tremble in her voice, and she wondered if Thomas heard it too. "I mean, your people marry young, right?"

∽

Thomas wasn't going to tell her that he couldn't picture himself with anyone but her. It was an impossible situation. Even if she wasn't going off to school, one of them would have to overhaul their life for them to be together.

"Everyone doesn't marry young. Some people are even close to thirty, but *ya* . . . between eighteen and twenty-two are when most people get baptized and married." He glanced her way, happy to be hiding his eyes behind his own dark sunglasses he'd slipped on. Maybe she wouldn't see the hurt he felt in his eyes at the thought of not being with her. "I don't think I'll be a man who marries young."

"Why do you say that?" She poked him gently on the arm. "Remember, you said you're a pretty good guy, and I think so too."

From every indication he'd picked up on, Janelle liked him, and she might be falling for him just a little too. Was she fishing right now, wondering if they might have any kind of future together? He didn't think that was possible. Even if they wrote letters and spent time together when she came home to visit her folks, long distance relationships were hard to sustain . . . or so he had heard.

"What about you? Could you give up your car and modern conveniences to live the way we do?" Now it was Thomas who was fishing. If there was even the tiniest chance she could choose this life, he'd pray every night that she would choose the Amish way. It was a stretch though. She had four years of college in her plans. Janelle would grow and change and learn new things, and they'd likely grow apart. They'd write to each other at first, then the letters would come less and less, and she'd probably meet someone at her fancy new school.

"Yep, I sure could." She flashed a broad smile his way.

He laughed. "*Ya*, well, you sure answered fast without really thinking about it." But Thomas's heart swelled with hope.

"It's so peaceful here. And beautiful," she said in a wispy voice as she scanned the fields on either side of them, filled with lush greenery and fields of colorful wildflowers. None were as stunning as Fannie's place, but still pretty.

"Most *Englisch* can't make the change, even *gut* Christian folks who share our beliefs. Our ways are just too strict for them after having all the modern conveniences available to them."

"I admit, it would be hard to give up my car." She laughed. "Well, maybe not. I love riding in this buggy and being able to smell the flowers. You know what they say, people don't stop to smell the flowers enough. In the buggy, you can smell them during the entire journey." She shrugged. "I'd live here forever if I could. I don't even want to go to college, but my parents feel strongly that I should since I had several scholarship offers. But, if it was up to me, I'd stay here and help my mom run her store. And I'd have my own garden."

Thomas wanted Janelle to have everything she dreamed about, and if it was college and a career, then that's what he wanted for her. But this was the first time she'd ever said she didn't even want to go to college, and he was more hopeful than ever now. He decided right then and there to give this to God. If he and Janelle fell in love—something he still wasn't sure could happen over a few weeks—and were meant to be together, things would fall into place.

He slowed the buggy, then pulled over on the side of the back road they'd been traveling on. There were no houses in sight, just fields of greenery and flowers. He stepped out of the buggy and loosely tethered his horse to the post of a barbed wire fence nearby. She opened her door and got out, then eased around the buggy and stood next to him. Instinctively, he reached for her hand, then pointed upward with his other hand. "There it is."

She gasped and pushed her sunglasses atop her head again, despite the full force of the sun. Holding a hand to her forehead, she said, "There's an eagle up there. I thought you were just going to show me a massive nest but look at that! I've never seen one." She kept her eyes on the bird. "Is it a boy or a girl?"

Thomas was disappointed that she let go of his hand, but she brought it to her forehead next to the other one to help block the sun. He still had his sunglasses on since he couldn't stop staring at her, and it was easier to watch her without her knowing.

"I don't know. If there were two eagles up there, we might be able to tell the gender because females are about a third larger than the males. But they don't have any distinctive features to tell them apart the way cardinals do – the pretty red ones are the males and the ones less colorful are the females."

She sighed, slipped her sunglasses back down on her nose, and said, "Yeah, and that's just wrong. I think God should have made the red cardinals the female ones."

It took him a couple of seconds to recall a word she

had used, and he hoped he used it in the right context. "That's a bit chauvinistic, isn't it?"

She laughed. "I guess so." After lifting her eyes to the big bird again, she said, "Wow. Just amazing."

You're amazing.

"Oh. I almost forgot something." She reached into the pocket of her blue jeans and pulled out the black leather bracelet she hadn't worn since she'd stopped wearing all black. "Remember when I said that I wore this to remind me that violence wasn't the answer?"

Thomas hung his head. "I'm not proud of what I did." Then he took off his sunglasses, stared at her few a couple of seconds, then gently reached for hers and removed them. He locked eyes with her. "But I would do it again if you were in danger."

"I know you would, but I hope you are never put in a situation like that again." She handed him the bracelet. He noticed she wasn't wearing black fingernail polish. "I don't know if you're allowed to wear it, but . . ." She shrugged. "I want you to have it." She turned it over as he held it. "It has an inscription on the inside."

Thomas leaned closer to read what had been etched into the leather band. He had to get really close to read the small words that ran the length of the thick band: *My God, my rock, in whom I take refuge, my shield and horn of my salvation, my stronghold and my refuge; my Savior, You save me from violence.*

He swallowed the lump forming in his throat. Thomas had sensed that Janelle was a spiritual person, but he had no idea how much so, and despite the heat, a cool ripple ran the length of his spine. "Samuel 22:3. It's one of my favorite verses in the Bible, something we strongly believe in." He hung his head as shame wrapped around him again. And he'd just told Janelle that he would protect her in the same manner all over again if he had to. Even though he'd asked the Lord for forgiveness, his doubts about himself swirled in his mind.

She touched his arm. "Thomas, I know you feel badly about hitting Brian. I feel horrible that you were even in that situation, but God uses everything we do for good, even when we mess up." She gently took the bracelet from his hand, then snapped it around his wrist. "You can take it off before you get home. It served as a reminder to me not to lose my cool. Maybe you can keep it in a drawer in your bedroom or something." She shrugged. "Maybe you'll think about God and pray that I'm protected without any acts of violence, and I can pray the same for you."

"I will wear it and never take it off." Thomas's voice cracked, so he cleared his throat. "*Danki*, if you're sure you . . ."

She smiled. "I'm sure. But I don't want you to get in trouble for wearing it."

He shook his head. "I won't. I'm in *mei rumschpringe*, my running around time. We're allowed a few liberties."

They were quiet for a few seconds as they stood on the side of the road "Can I ask you something?" He gingerly ran a finger around the leather band that was snapped around his wrist.

She chewed her bottom lip and hesitated. "Um, sure."

"You look so pretty without all that dark makeup, the

black clothes, and boots, and all that. Are you going to dress that way again when you go to college?"

With her sunglasses still atop her head, she met his gaze. "No, I'm not. Our friendship has helped me to see myself from the inside out."

"So, you're a butterfly now?" He brushed wild strands of hair from her face.

She shook her head. "No. I'm not." She stared at him. "Not yet." Pausing, she blinked back tears. "Maybe I never will be. But our friendship is special, and I feel like I'm getting to know myself better when I'm around you." She lowered her head, but Thomas cupped her chin and brought her eyes back to his.

"Our friendship is special to me too." He was going to take his shot. "And if you weren't leaving, I'd be hoping for more than just friendship."

A tear rolled down her cheek. "We can never be more than friends."

"I know." *I'm Amish, and you're not.*

He wiped away the tear with his thumb. "We can be *best* friends then." He could feel tiny cracks in his heart. How and why had he let this girl—woman—get into his heart this way when they had no possibility of a future together?

She smiled. "Best friends forever."

Thomas returned the smile . . . even though his heart was breaking.

CHAPTER 11

Janelle laughed every time she hit a pothole on the road to Fannie's house. She'd been driving the buggy for the past few weeks, and she would miss it when she left for college. "Why is it that I seem to hit every pothole on these backroads?" She hit another one, and Thomas bounced so hard in his seat that his head bumped the top of the buggy. "Sorry." She cringed.

He laughed, something else she would miss . . . the sound of his voice, his laughter, the gentle way he held her hand sometimes. His eye had healed completely though there was a scar above his right eye. He said it would be a reminder to avoid violence, and he told her he hadn't taken off the leather band since she'd given it to him, except when he bathed so he didn't ruin it.

"If you pull the reins just a little bit one way or the other, you can get the horse to maneuver around those holes." He chuckled when she tried but hit another crater in the road. "When you come home to visit, we can work on that part."

She stayed quiet. During their outings, they had mostly avoided conversations about her leaving.

"*Ach*, and don't forget to give me your address so I can write to you at school."

She took a deep breath in an effort not to cry before she spoke. "I don't know my address at school yet. Why don't you just give me yours? I'll know what dorm I'm in when my parents take me there."

Thomas nodded as Janelle turned on the road to Fannie's house. This would be her last time to dance with the butterflies until they returned next year. If they were still here in late fall, like Thomas said they were sometimes, she could sneak over unnoticed and spend time in this special place. But for today, the beauty of the wildflowers and butterflies would become special for another reason.

She slowed the horse to a complete stop, and Thomas jumped out and tethered it to the fence. Then he took her hand as they made their way to the field, surely one of God's special places too. "What about snakes?" she asked as she lifted her legs high. She hadn't really thought about snakes during her first visit. But Thomas hadn't mentioned snakes until they went to the pond at the abandoned house.

He squatted down.

She put her hands on her hips. "What are you doing?"

"Jump on my back." He motioned with his hands. "Come on. You can't weigh that much."

The thought of being that close to him caused her

heart to skip a beat. They had hugged two or three times when saying goodbye following a day of activities, but it had been awkward, as if they were both trying to hold firm to the friendship boundaries.

"Okay." She jumped on his back, and he stood with ease. "Now, nothing will get you." He laughed. Janelle wanted to cry—out of a mixture of heartbreak and joy. But then they arrived, and the display was equally as amazing as their first visit. It wasn't long before she waved her arms in the air, then stilled to let the beautiful creatures land on her. She felt silly that she'd thought about snakes here. This was a magical place where no harm could come to her.

When she finally stopped to catch her breath, she glanced at Thomas, and even with his sunglasses on, she suspected he was hiding pain. Not as much as hers though. He thought she would be visiting and spending time with him. She would come back to Montgomery for holidays and to visit her parents, but she wouldn't write to Thomas, nor visit him.

"You are so beautiful," he said as he shuffled through the flowers until he was standing right in front of her. "Is this the place? Am I the person?" he asked with a serious expression.

Janelle had saved herself for this moment. The few friends she'd had before the fire had kissed guys. She'd been too nervous at fourteen when her friends were having their first kisses to do the same. Here, though, her longing for Thomas was strong. He was everything she wanted in a man. She would be eighteen soon. Hadn't everyone had a sweet sixteen kiss? For her, it would be a first kiss and a goodbye kiss, and she hoped she could do it and not cry. "Yes," she whispered just as he cupped her cheeks with both hands, his heart-rendering gaze filled with tenderness.

There was a tingling in the pit of Janelle's stomach as his lips gently brushed against hers like the wings of the butterflies that encircled them with a protective halo of joy. Her pulse skittered as he pulled her close, and she felt his heart thudding against her own as one kiss led to another. Their kisses grew more intimate. Could he feel her heart breaking?

It was a first kiss that her soul melted into, and if she could wish for anything in the world, it would be for Thomas to love her.

As he withdrew from the kiss sooner than she would have liked, she drifted back down to earth from the soft and wispy cloud she'd been floating on. He gazed into her eyes with such intensity, her knees began to tremble.

"This will sound crazy, Janelle . . . because I know we haven't known each other that long, but . . . I love you." He kissed her again before she had time to respond.

Her emotions swirled with happiness, then skidded onto the path of reality. Even though she wanted to stay in his arms forever, she needed to guard her heart, if that was possible. He loved what he knew about her, not the disfiguring scars beneath her clothes.

"Was it everything you hoped for?" He tenderly kissed her on the cheek.

She needed to take things down a notch even though it broke her heart to do so. "I'm glad my first kiss was with my best friend, and yes, it was everything I had hoped for, and more."

If he was waiting for her to say she loved him too, he didn't let on. Surely, it had to be on his mind. Her heart ached with a deep longing to tell him she loved him, but she couldn't.

∽

THOMAS WAS ACUTELY aware that she hadn't returned the sentiment. Maybe she didn't love him, or wasn't sure, or didn't want to say it because she was leaving in a couple of days. Maybe she would say it before she left for school. Whatever her reason, he wasn't going to say it again, and he was going to try not to overanalyze it. *That might be impossible.*

He took her hand in his, and they slowly started back to the buggy. The ability to avoid overanalyzing wasn't working, and it was becoming heavier on his heart with each step, even though he worked to convince himself that people couldn't fall in love this quickly, in a matter of weeks.

"Do you mind driving me home in the buggy?" She let go of his hand, then swiped at wayward strands of damp hair that had come loose from her ponytail. "I am dripping in sweat, and all that dancing around wore me out." She tried to laugh, but it wasn't a real laugh. There was still a lot of daylight left. She was cutting short their time together.

"I don't mind," he said as he untethered the horse.

When she hadn't said anything for a while, he finally asked her what was wrong.

Her chest rose and fell as she took a deep breath. Her sunglasses kept him from seeing any emotion in her eyes, but she turned to him and said, "I'm sad."

She'd already told him the kiss was great, so she had to be sad she was leaving in a couple of days. "*Ya*, I'm sad too." He waited, but she just hung her head. "Well, at least we've got tomorrow to spend the day together," he finally said.

Silence.

"Janelle, what's going on?" His heart pounded in his chest.

"I'm leaving tonight. My parents got a hotel in Indianapolis, and we're scheduled to tour the campus tomorrow, and I'll be staying. I guess I got my days mixed up."

He wondered if that was true. "Oh," he said dryly.

They were quiet the rest of the way to her house. She might as well have been wearing her black clothes and makeup again. But even when she'd dressed like that, she'd been chipper and talkative. She'd said she was sad. Maybe that's what all the silence was about.

When he pulled the buggy to a stop, he said, "I'm going to miss you."

Surprisingly, she threw herself into his arms and started to cry. "I thought I could do this without crying, but I'm going to miss you too." As her tears commingled with the sweat on his shirt, he stroked her hair. "I thought it would be easiest to make a clean break without a bunch of emotional . . . you know?"

Thank you, God. She didn't say she loved him, but she

was going to miss him. He held her, kissed her several times on the forehead, then she finally dried her eyes.

"I better go in." She bit her lip, blinking back tears as she gazed into his eyes.

Just say it . . . tell me you love me too.

"The kiss was more than I could have dreamed of, and this has been the best summer of my life." She sniffled. "I will miss you very much."

"*Ach*, I almost forgot . . . I need to give you my address." He looked around for something to write with, then glanced at her purse on the floorboard of the buggy. "Do you have a pen and paper in there?"

"Uh, yes." She reached down, picked up her purse, then handed him a small pad of paper and a pen, and he quickly scribbled his address. After he handed her the paper, and after another long kiss—the final goodbye kiss—she turned and ran toward her house.

Thomas slowly headed home. With a hole in his heart.

∽

Janelle ran past her parents in the living room and darted up the stairs. Her mother called after her, but she didn't answer. After flinging herself on the bed, she buried her head in her pillow and sobbed.

A gentle hand landed on her back. "I know how much you care about that boy," her mother said. "And I was afraid this would happen, Honey. But even if you weren't going away to school, what chance would the two of you have? Unless you were willing to convert to his way of life, or he was willing to change his ways, it just wouldn't have worked."

Janelle rolled onto her back, her sadness morphing into anger. "I love him, Mom. And maybe you think I'm too young to be in love, but I am."

"Sweetheart, I met your dad when I was your age. Granted, we didn't get married for another four years, but I do understand that the heart wants what the heart wants." She sighed. "But with Thomas being Amish, it's a whole new ballgame. And when you get to school, you'll meet someone else, and eventually the sting will heal."

"Thomas told me he loved me." Janelle heard the curtness in her voice. She and her mother were close, and in many ways, her mom was her best friend.

"Oh, Honey." Her mother hung her head. "I know that's hard to walk away from."

"Easier than you think." She sat up, grabbed the collar of her pink shirt, and ripped down, tearing each button off. Only her bra was exposed to her mother, along with the longtime scars that ran from right above her breasts all the way past her elbows. Splotches here and there weren't scarred, but her ivory skin was tarnished. "No one is ever going to love this! No one, Mom! Ever!"

There was a knock at the door.

"Don't come in, Roger. Everything is fine."

Her mother put a hand on Janelle's upper chest. "This is what Thomas fell in love with, your heart." She dropped her hand to her stomach. "And these scars don't define your beauty, Janelle. I've never known anyone as caring, loving, protective, strong, and brave as you."

Janelle rolled her eyes. "You're my mom. You have to

say that." She put her hand on top of her mother's. "But seriously, Mom . . . no man is going to want to be with me, a scarred-up version of someone who used to be halfway decent looking."

Her mother shook her head. "You're wrong." She said it so firmly that Janelle almost—or at the least—wanted to believe her. "I'm so proud that you ditched all that black makeup and started wearing more colorful clothes. And, yes, I think we probably have Thomas to credit for that. You trusted him enough to let him see the real you, but it doesn't have anything to do with clothes or makeup. Thomas saw your heart. And you let him, something you haven't been willing to do since the fire."

"I pray. I thank God all the time for not taking my life. I don't blame God. I don't blame anyone." She started to cry again. "But I don't understand how God would let this happen to me."

"God doesn't let things happen to people. I believe He interjects when He can for the good of a situation. God sees your true beauty. Your father and I see it. And Thomas saw it." She stood up and pointed a finger at Janelle. "Maybe you didn't give that young man enough credit."

"You didn't see the way he looked at me, Mom. There was so much love and passion in his eyes. That's how I want to remember him, and how I want him to remember me."

"Come downstairs when you're ready. But I'm telling you . . . the right person will love everything about you. We are all flawed, and in my opinion, in many ways it's better to be flawed on the outside and not on the inside.

And you, my dear . . . a person would have to search hard to find your flaws on the inside. Love yourself the way God loves you, and the right person will latch on to that with every part of their being."

She blew her a kiss, then gently closed the door.

Janelle closed her eyes to memorize Thomas's face, the kisses, and every conversation they'd ever had. But the tears came even harder and faster.

CHAPTER 12

*T*homas waited six weeks before he stopped in at Janelle's mother's store. It was a desperate move, but he felt like a desperate man. Not one letter from Janelle. He'd either misread her completely, she saw him as nothing more than a summer distraction, or she'd met someone right away at school. Whatever it was, he couldn't stand not knowing. The bell on the door jingled as he entered the store.

"Thomas." Janelle's mother stopped dead in her tracks holding a small box of books. "Lovely to see you." She smiled, but there was no mistaking her surprise as she raised an eyebrow. "Everything okay?"

He removed his hat, glanced around the store, then said, "I didn't see any cars or buggies outside . . . I mean, besides your car, and I wondered if this might be a *gut* time to talk to you."

"Of course. It's near closing time, so I doubt I'll have any more customers." She carried the small box to the counter by the front door, then maneuvered around to a stool on the other side after setting the books down. "What's on your mind?"

"Um . . . I was just wondering about Janelle." He felt his face turning red. "She said she was going to write to me, but I haven't heard, and . . ." He cleared his throat. "Is she okay?"

Sharlene lowered her head for a moment, then looked back up at him. "She's fine, Thomas. And I know she regrets the way things ended up."

He shuffled a work boot against the tile floor as he looked down. "Does she have a boyfriend already?"

"No." Sharlene didn't hesitate.

Thomas scratched his head. "I just don't get it. I thought we were friends, and I'm confused why she hasn't written."

Janelle's mother smiled. "You're not friends. You're two people who fell in love."

Thomas's heart rate spiked. "Did she say that, that she loved me?" He couldn't breathe as he waited for an answer.

"Yes. She did." Sharlene walked around the corner and returned with a stool like the one she'd been perched on. "You might want to sit down."

"*Ach*, this can't be *gut*." He sat, his hat in his lap to hide his trembling hands.

"There is one thing you shouldn't doubt, and that's the fact that Janelle does love you, and she knows you love her."

"Then why isn't she writing me?" His voice was louder than he intended.

Sharlene sighed. "She felt like a clean break would be

the easiest thing for both of you. And Thomas . . . how could a romantic relationship work between the two of you when you are Amish, and she isn't?"

"I don't know, but I would have liked to have found out." He forced the bitterness he felt aside and tried to focus on the fact that she loved him. At least, she had told her mother she did. "Sometimes people convert, one way or the other. But, no matter what, I thought we were close enough that she wouldn't cut all ties." His voice cracked toward the end of the sentence, and he looked away from Sharlene, his face feeling hot again.

"Hon, I know you're hurting. Janelle is too. I tried to get her to talk to you."

He was quiet, unsure what to say.

Sharlene tapped a finger to her chin. "You really do love her, don't you?"

He nodded. "I know we didn't know each other long, but *ya*, I do. And maybe it wouldn't have worked out, but I'm . . ." his voice trailed off as he avoided Sharlene's eyes again.

"Tell me what you love about her." Sharlene tipped her head to one side.

He looked up. "Everything. Her free spirit, her kindness, she's gentle, but strong. She's smart, she's beautiful. I could go on and on."

"Have you heard the saying that beauty is in the eye of the beholder?"

Thomas nodded.

"Janelle is all those things you mentioned . . . and a lot more. But she doesn't see herself as beautiful on the outside, thus all the dark makeup and clothes when you first met her. But as she started to trust you and be more comfortable in her own skin, she began to change. But she couldn't quite be the butterfly she wanted to be and began to withdraw again, even if only on the inside."

"I don't understand." Thomas sighed. "She told me about wanting to morph into something beautiful like a butterfly. I thought she had."

"Oh boy." Sharlene closed her eyes and shook her head. "Janelle is going to kill me."

"What?" Thomas sensed that maybe answers were coming his way.

"Three years ago, our house caught on fire. It started as an electrical fire and spread quickly. Janelle's father and I weren't home, but she was napping after school, so she was in the house. She was rescued from her totally engulfed bedroom by a fireman who came through the window and pulled her out of the room, then immediately rolled her in the grass." Sharlene paused as she blinked back tears. "Thomas, Janelle was burned from her chest almost all the way to her ankles and down to past her elbows. She's undergone many painful surgeries and skin grafts, and maybe there will be more down the line, but she will always have those scars covering most of her body. Only me and her doctors have seen all her scars. She won't even let her father see them all."

Thomas was speechless, but not for long. "I don't care about that. I love the person Janelle is inside."

Sharlene covered her face and wept. "I told her a person would come along who would love her for that very reason." She sniffled, then locked eyes with him, her lips pressed firmly together for a few seconds. "You're young, Thomas. There are a lot of mature men much older than you who would run from something like that."

He stood. "I'm not one of them."

Janelle's mother smiled as a tear rolled down her cheek. "I didn't think you were. But now you know why she left so abruptly and ceased communication. It wasn't fair to you, and that's why I told you. I don't want you to spend the rest of your life thinking you loved someone who didn't love you back."

He sat again, hung his head. "*Danki* for telling me. But I don't care what she looks like on the outside."

Sharlene sighed again. "Of course, you do. You were drawn to her beautiful face as well as her beautiful heart. You wouldn't be normal if this news didn't cause you even a little discomfort."

"*Ya*, I'm shocked. But I got to know the real Janelle, the butterfly waiting to be set free, to know herself, to love herself, to love . . . me . . . I thought."

Sharlene tucked her blonde hair behind her ears and smiled. "She's coming home this weekend."

"I thought she wasn't coming home until Thanksgiving." Thomas felt a surge of hope spring to life as his heart pumped faster.

"She's already been home once, I'm sorry to tell you, but she didn't feel it best to see you, as I said before."

"Why are you telling me now?"

"Because you have a right to know her true feelings. What you both decide to do with those feelings is up to you. Even if her scars don't bother you, there are a lot of other issues at play since she isn't Amish."

"I know."

Sharlene seemed like she wanted to say more, but every time she opened her mouth to speak, she closed it again.

"We don't judge people by their looks though," Thomas said firmly. "I would be lying if I said I wasn't a little nervous to see what the fire did to her, but I know it won't change *mei* feelings for her."

"I appreciate that admission, Thomas. I don't think you'd be normal if you weren't having those thoughts."

"I was raised not to be judgmental, and I understand that we still are drawn to people due to physical attraction, but things were . . . different . . . with Janelle. She's special."

Sharlene smiled. "Her father and I certainly think so."

Thomas tried to envision in his mind the worst possible scars covering Janelle's body, grotesque disfigurations, and it still didn't change the way he felt about her. "I'm guessing she won't want to see me during her visit this weekend."

"Probably not."

Sharlene rubbed her forehead, seemingly in deep concentration, then she looked across the counter at Thomas. "She is afraid the Monarch butterflies will be gone by Thanksgiving. And she wants to see them one last time before they leave so she doesn't have to wait another year. She told me they are most active around two in the afternoon." She paused, a slight smile on her face. "That's where you can find her on Saturday. She said it's a magical place, that the Monarchs land on her, and that it helps to heal her heart. She asked me to go with her, but I'm going to bow out now."

"Will she be mad you told me everything?" Thomas already knew he would be in Fannie's meadow at two on Saturday, but he hated that Sharlene might be in trouble for sharing with him.

Janelle's mother shrugged. "Probably. But I'm going to trust that everything you told me is the truth, and if there is even a chance that there is truly magic in the meadow, I'm going to put my faith in you."

Thomas stood, put on his hat, and nodded. "There is magic, and it comes from *Gott* in the form of divine blessings. And I believe the Monarchs are a gift from Him."

"There's one more thing . . ." Sharlene waved a dismissive hand. "Never mind. Go see Janelle on Saturday. It will either go well, or I'll take my verbal lashing when she gets home."

Thomas smiled. "I don't think you'll have to worry about that. Everything is going to be fine."

∼

JANELLE PARKED her car as close to the meadow as she could get. When she glanced at the porch, Fannie wasn't outside, so she made her trek into the meadow, no longer concerned about snakes. At least, not here. She saw the Monarchs in the distance amidst the colorful blooms, and she could already feel them soothing her soul. Her broken heart would take more time to heal.

She had on jeans, tennis shoes, and a short-sleeve red T-shirt since she'd read that butterflies were attracted to red. She took off her blue jean jacket and tossed it to the ground. Her scars from her elbows up were visible for the first time to the butterflies. She held out her arms, closed her eyes, and leaned her head back. Within seconds the beautiful Monarchs swirled around her, several landing on her upper arms. A cool breeze rustled the flowers, then blew through her hair. *Lord, I know it isn't in Your will to change my appearance, but I'm begging You to heal my heart, to make me whole on the inside.*

She was lost in thought and prayer, but when her peripheral vision caught some movement coming toward her, she dropped her arms, gasped, then put a hand over her mouth. "Thomas. What are you doing here?" She spun frantically in circles searching for her jacket. But after he moved closer, his fingertips grazing her skin. She jerked away from him, doing her best to cover her arms with her hands until she finally located her jacket and picked it up.

"I didn't hear your buggy." She awkwardly tried to get the light jacket on even though she'd felt such freedom without it.

Thomas paused her movements by stepping close to her, laying his hand atop hers to bring it down. "It's okay." Her jacket slipped from her hand, then landed at her feet.

Janelle covered her face with her hands and sobbed. "Please don't look at me."

She trembled when she felt his hands cup her elbows before gingerly running his hands up her arms and beneath the sleeves of her T-shirt, all the way up to her shoulders.

"Please stop." He was so tender, and there was love in his touch. She could feel it, but she couldn't bring herself to look into his eyes, afraid his gaze would reveal what he really thought. She would relive this moment in her mind for the rest of her life.

He gently cupped her chin, forcing her to look up at him. He smiled, brushed the tears from her cheeks with his thumbs, then kissed her with even more passion than the last time, and she allowed herself to get swept up in the love she felt for him.

After he eased away, Thomas rubbed her arms. "Is this why you ran away from me? From us?"

She tried to lower her eyes, but once again, he gently lifted her chin until she was facing him, his hands still running the length of her arms.

Sniffling, she said, "Thomas, most of my body looks like this."

"So?"

She jerked out of his arms and cried. "How can you say that? *So?* Did you hear what I said?"

Thomas walked to her and gently held her shoulders. "Did you hear what I said when I said I loved you?"

"But you haven't seen—?"

He put a finger to her lips, then brought one of her arms to his mouth and gently kissed her above the elbow, tenderly, like the brush of a butterfly's wings. Repeatedly, his mouth trailed her scars as the Monarchs circled them, but there was no magic in the air, only the Holy Spirit. When he finally looked up at her, he raised an eyebrow.

"Do you have something to tell me?"

She nodded as tears trailed down her face, but on the inside, she'd been transformed. "I love you," she breathed.

He rubbed her arms again, then pulled her close to him, and kissed her. "It's about time you told me."

She smiled. "But I didn't want to stick you with—"

"Stop," he said. "I've found the person I want to be with. Now enjoy being with me too."

She was quickly quieted when his lips found hers again. And she couldn't stop smiling.

Thomas smiled too. "Now, there's *mei* butterfly, *ya?*"

Janelle was smiling on the inside, and for once, her entire being was smiling on the outside. "I'm your butterfly."

He ran his finger down the nape of her neck before he cupped her cheeks and kissed her again. "Hello butterfly."

She didn't know how God would see things through for her and Thomas, but for now, she was content knowing he loved her . . . all of her.

EPILOGUE

Janelle put her hands on her hips. She was still getting used to long dresses and black aprons, but she loved going barefoot, the plush grass tickling her toes. After staring at her and Thomas's house, she twirled the string on her prayer covering in between her fingers.

"Who would have ever thought this place would be a home again?"

Her husband sidled up next to her. "Remember when we had our picnic, the first time we were here?" There had been dozens of trips to the old farmstead since then.

"I'll never forget it. You punched Brian Edwards."

Thomas cringed. "*Ya*, I try not to think about that part."

"I think of it as *Gott's* way of turning something bad into something *gut*. If we hadn't come here, I never would have envisioned this house as truly becoming a home again and housing a family."

Thomas eased his way behind her and wrapped his

arms around her enlarged belly. "And our little family of two is about to increase."

Janelle couldn't wait to be a mother, and she prayed she would be as good of a mom as her own mother.

She hadn't gone back to school after her visit with Thomas in the meadow, but she did finish some of her classes online—the ones related to horticulture. And she helped her mother at the store. To her surprise, her parents didn't fight her about not returning to school. They just wanted her to be happy. They were almost as accommodating, when months later, Janelle told them that she wanted to be baptized into the Amish faith and marry Thomas. But they'd convinced her and Thomas—along with Thomas's parents—to wait until the following fall. His parents said that was when weddings took place. Her parents said that they should take time to make sure they were both ready for such a large commitment.

Janelle had been ready that day in the meadow but waiting gave them time to purchase the old farmstead at a bargain price. They'd had lots of help from both of their families getting it turned into a beautiful home, just in time to welcome this new family member. And she'd put her skills in horticulture to good use and planted a stunning garden.

Fannie had passed on last summer, and a lovely English couple had purchased her farm. The Monarchs had arrived at the end of June, when the couple had scheduled their first visit. Janelle and Thomas had planned to keep their promise to Fannie, with the couple's permission, and keep plenty of native flowers for the butterflies. As it turned out, the couple saw the magic and felt the peace of God's hands on them out in the meadow, and they promised to make sure to replenish the seeds so the Monarchs would always return.

Fannie's place would always be special, but Janelle and Thomas planned to follow in their friend's footsteps and planted native flowers in a meadow of their own. Janelle pictured her children running through the field, flinging their arms in the air, and feeling the magic that only the presence of God could create.

∽

AND FOR THE next sixty-plus years, she never saw a snake.

A REQUEST

Authors depend on reviews from readers. If you enjoyed this book, would you please consider leaving a review on Amazon?

TURN THE PAGE . . .

. . . to read a note from the author and the first chapter of the bestselling novella, *The Messenger,* which was inspired by actual events.

A NOTE FROM THE AUTHOR ABOUT THE MESSENGER

The Messenger is a work of fiction, but I have yet to speak to an author who didn't incorporate life events into his or her books. I've penned over fifty books, and each one of my stories contains at least one element that represents an event in my life. *The Messenger* is no exception, and it is inspired by a true story.

My main character—Walter, his real name—was a man I met at a speaking event. He approached me after I had finished talking and explained to me how he had died and gone to heaven, but God sent him back to deliver messages to random people. He said he had a message for me from God. I was speaking at an assisted living facility, and Walter was up in age, so I was skeptical that God had sent him to deliver any words of wisdom for me. Then he said something profound, about an issue that was heavy on my heart, and he provided me with an answer from God. There was no way that this kind elderly man could have known what was at the core of my discomfort at that time in my life, and it brought me to tears.

I honestly don't know what happened to Walter, or if he is still alive, since this happened years ago. *The Messenger* has been percolating in my mind for a long time, and I'm happy to finally have the story available for readers. Keep an open mind. Be alert to the many ways our lives intersect to do God's will. Isn't that what life is about? Making a positive difference during our time here?

I hope you enjoy *The Messenger* and what it represents, even though it is a fictional project. God always works toward our best interests . . . and sometimes we have no way of knowing His plan until it falls into our lap in the form of good news . . . or maybe even a miracle.

Blessings to all of you,
    Beth

THE MESSENGER - PROLOGUE

Dying is a beautiful thing, especially at my age when the body no longer functions the way it should. I suffered through decades of arthritis that made me want to take a jackhammer to my knees. Then, a heart attack, two bypasses, esophageal cancer, and a life-threatening case of pneumonia almost took me down, but in the end, it was a bee sting. Yep, that's right—a wicked case of anaphylactic shock, which left me gasping for air on my living room floor until my granddaughter found me and rushed me to the emergency room. I was more than ready to go at age eighty-two when I heard that monitor flatline, knowing I'd soon see my beloved Mary Grace and my daughter, Lydia, who had passed away much too young. Cancer plagued our family, and I always assumed that's how I would go. Or maybe heart failure. My ticker wasn't what it should be, either. A bee sting wouldn't have been in my top one hundred causes of death.

Leaving my earthly existence happened as I had imagined, although the white light was a mixture of brilliant hues that I believe must have included every color in the rainbow, heavy on golden shades of yellow. I saw Mary Grace as my soul left my worn-out body on the hospital bed. She looked the same as the day I married her—tight blonde curls, a dimply smile, and sapphire eyes that lit up a room. Her presence immediately left me wondering what I looked like. Was I now the handsome young lad she'd married fifty-eight years ago? Or had I ascended into the next life as my slumped-over gray-haired self who walked with a limp?

Lydia was a beautiful woman in her twenties, cancer-free and glowing with good health. I was filled with a love I'd never felt as I glided along the well-lit path. It was like levitating barely off the ground toward a destiny that would forever fill me with contentment and peace.

If there was a downside to exiting my earthly existence, it was my granddaughter—Amelia—whom I was leaving behind. A woman in her early forties raising a troubled son. Amelia was good to me right up until the end, and I worried for her and Michael, her only child. The boy had been in and out of juvenile detention centers and had already caused his mother a lifetime of heartache by the age of seventeen.

But even my anxiety about leaving them wasn't enough to pull me from the euphoric state of mind that lured me toward my departed loved ones. I had waited for this moment to lay eyes on my family, to glide toward them without having any pain. Mary Grace was the first to greet me, wrapping her arms around me, no words necessary, as I could feel her every emotion radiate through my being. I was home.

Lydia was the next person to welcome me, and again, no words were needed. In the distance, I saw my parents, my brother Edwin, coworkers I remembered warmly, friends and neighbors who had come home before me, and other folks I hadn't seen in decades but of whom I had fond recollections. They'd all been waiting for me, and it was a reunion like no other. Again, it was everything I had imagined, short of one thing. I was hungry. Famished. I searched for a glorious spread of food that might be laid out by my welcoming party, but all I saw in front of me was the rainbow of lights and my family and friends.

My stomach growled, which seemed odd. I was in Heaven, but apparently there was food in Heaven, or I wouldn't be feeling this mild annoyance. I wondered if I would eventually be offered a juicy red steak complemented by a fully loaded baked potato. Perhaps even a slice of red velvet cake loaded with cream cheese icing and a side of vanilla ice cream. My favorites, but the food I'd steered away from since Amelia had insisted that I partake in a heart-healthy diet.

Flanked by family and friends, I kept floating toward the golden gates, and as I neared, they opened with ease, and a new sort of light met me on the other side. I knew immediately what—and who—the light was, and I dropped to my knees and lowered my head, unworthy to face the Son of God or even be in His presence. I wept with feelings of gratitude and remorse over things I'd done in my life, but I mostly absorbed His love like a sponge that had been dry until this moment in time.

My family and friends dispersed before I was ready for them to go, but I suppose this was the point when I faced all my wrongdoings head-on, begged to be absolved of my sins, and embraced my Lord and Savior with all the love in my heart. But my stomach wouldn't stop growling, which was a distraction at the very least.

When a hand cupped my chin and eased me to my feet, I stood and gazed upon Jesus. I instinctively embraced Him. Every sin I'd ever committed slapped me in the face like a wet rag, unpleasant but not hurtful. I wanted to stay in His arms forever, but when my stomach grumbled even louder, I knew something was amiss. Jesus asked me to walk with Him, although it wasn't really walking. It was like skating without skates, not gliding or floating. It was different than earlier.

Jesus communicated to me without speaking, and I knew that ahead of me was God. Nothing in my life could have prepared me for this moment, and the peaceful calm I'd always envisioned wrapped around me like a blanket of bliss, perfect in every way. Except for my hunger pains, which continued to confuse me.

As I took a seat next to my Heavenly Father, I couldn't remember the last time I'd sat without my knees throbbing with pain. I was especially grateful for the Lord's mercy and my pain-free new existence.

God began to communicate with me using words. His voice was deep, which might have sounded threatening if He hadn't been who He was. Or perhaps I had been wrong in my assumptions. Maybe I should have felt threatened. I hadn't done anything awful, like kill anyone or intentionally cause harm to another person, but I'd committed my fair share of sins. Despite the love I felt, I braced myself for what was to come. All the while, visions of steak and baked potatoes filled my senses with guilt, knowing I shouldn't be thinking of such things right now.

"Walter, I've been waiting for you," God said in His deep voice. "You're very special to me."

I swallowed hard, surprised that, despite my painless existence, I had a lump in my throat. It was accompanied by the guilt I felt as I wondered if He said that to everyone. Or was I really special? God smiled. I think.

"But you can't stay." God spoke firmly, and tears welled at the corners of my eyes. Had I miscalculated my misdeeds? Was I going to the other place instead?

"Why?" My voice sounded like that of a child pleading with his mother about why he couldn't go to the playground or something equally as unmatched as this conversation.

"There are things I need you to do before you take permanent residence here." God spoke firmly, but I'd never been so relieved in my life. At least I would be returning. But I stiffened and said the first thing that came to mind.

"I don't want to go back. I want to stay here." Was this going to be a debate? Was I expected to plead my case? I felt sure I would lose for all the obvious reasons.

"I know you don't want to leave, but it is necessary." God placed a soothing hand on my shoulder. "You will return to your earthly home with renewed health, and you will hear My voice in your mind, directing you to do My will."

"Huh?" I tried to swallow that lump in my throat again as I blinked back tears. *Why me?*

"There are those who cannot—or choose not to—hear My voice. They have blocked My guidance in their lives out of fear, worry, anxiety, or disbelief. But I love all My children, and I want to save as many as I can."

I wanted to ask God how I factored into what He was saying, but I knew right away that He knew what I was thinking.

"When you return in the grandest of health, you will meet people who need to hear what I have to say in order to find their way to Me. I will guide you in this endeavor. Just listen for My voice the way you always have."

How many times had I felt the Lord guiding me? Is that what He meant?

"Yes," He said right away. "You will find yourself in situations, often with strangers, that will require you to spread My messages in an effort to help that person shed the suffering he or she is feeling, to forgo their fears, and to seek Me with all their heart."

My stomach growled loudly, and I was sure the Lord heard it rumbling. "How long do I get to stay here?" A tear trickled down my cheek as I wondered how much time I would have with Mary Grace and Lydia.

"No time at all. You will go back right away."

My heart sank to my tormented stomach, which clenched as I fought the urge to openly sob.

"I will see you again, My son." God spoke softer this

time, His voice still deep and filled with love, but He felt my pain. I was sure of it.

There was no point in arguing, begging to stay. I knew I was going back.

And it happened instantly. I was back in the hospital bed when I opened my eyes, but all was quiet. No monitors beeping, noisy oxygen machine, or doctors scrambling to bring me back to life. Only Amelia. My granddaughter had her back to me as her shoulders shook from crying. I'd been pronounced dead, and presumably, Amelia had been given some time alone with me to grieve.

It occurred to me that I had encountered some sort of near-death experience. Had it all been a dream? I took a deep breath—a deep, full breath like I hadn't taken in years, as if my lungs were that of a healthy twenty-year-old. The aches and pains that consumed most of my body seemed to have fled as I moved slightly in the bed. But it was my knees that spoke to me in an unfamiliar language. They moved and shifted with ease, and I chuckled.

Amelia spun around so fast she backed into a tray filled with medical supplies that went toppling to the floor. As her jaw dropped, my granddaughter looked like she'd seen a ghost before she bolted from the room, screaming for a doctor.

Moments later, three doctors and a nurse came rushing into the room. Amelia stood in the background yelling, "Grandpa, can you hear me? Grandpa?" I'd also been hard of hearing for over a decade.

I waved my arms around so everyone would stop hovering over me and checking my vitals and poking and prodding me. I'd had enough of all that. "Stop! Just stop!" I said with more anger than I had intended. But would all that touching by mere mortals cause my pain to return? I couldn't chance it.

A young doctor, although probably the oldest person in the room, leaned down close to me and said loudly, "Walter, can you hear me?"

"Yes." Frustration fueled the taut strain in my voice. "And there is something I *need*."

"What's that?" The doctor asked, still much too loud for my liking. I glanced back and forth between me and the machine by the bed that was now beeping in a steady rhythm.

"I need a steak, preferably ribeye, medium rare, and a fully loaded baked potato with extra sour cream. A salad would be nice, too, and I'd like blue cheese dressing." I paused, my mouth watering as I envisioned the meal. "And a slice of red velvet cake topped with vanilla ice cream, please."

Amelia was quickly by my side, inching the doctors out of the way. "Grandpa, I love you so much. I thought we'd lost you." She kissed me on the forehead.

I opened my mouth to tell her that she had lost me for a while, but I knew my story would sound crazy.

My granddaughter turned to the doctor and said, "Maybe we should get him some pudding or yogurt or something easy on his stomach."

I growled. "Amelia, I love you. But if someone doesn't round me up a steak, I'm going to rip all these tubes from my arms and get it myself." And I was pretty sure I could.

I regretted my harsh outburst right away, but people started moving quickly after that, checking my vitals and visibly scanning me from head to toe. Amelia promised to take me to my favorite steakhouse, so I practiced patience, which was difficult. My stomach was grumbling, but even more so . . . my life had changed. Something was on the horizon, which felt exhilarating and terrifying at the same time.

THE MESSENGER - CHAPTER ONE

Walter savored the taste of his ribeye as his granddaughter gazed at him across the table, her bottom lip trembling slightly. Amelia was likely still in shock. She'd seen her grandfather die, then come back to life like something out of a sci-fi movie.

"I'm not saying that I don't believe you, Grandpa, but you have to admit . . . it's a lot to swallow." Amelia slouched into the booth seat as she folded her hands atop the table. Walter had told her everything as he remembered it.

After he finished the last bite of his steak, he laid his fork across his plate, undecided if he would order that slice of red velvet cake he'd been longing for. "You need to eat something." His granddaughter was too thin. Walter blamed a lot of that on his great-grandson. Michael kept his mother in a continuous state of worry. "And yes . . . I understand that my story is a lot to swallow." He had been questioning the reality of his tale ever since he'd awoken back in his hospital bed. But his lack of pain and bounce in his step was proof that he hadn't imagined the entire thing. He was skeptical about certain recollections though. Walter didn't think he'd ever really met a stranger, often striking up conversations at the grocery store with folks he didn't know, or at the post office, bank, or any public place. But this was different.

He recalled what God had asked him to do. *When you return in the grandest of health, you will meet people who need to hear what I have to say in order to find their way to Me. I will guide you in this endeavor. Just listen for My voice the way you always have.*

How would he deliver—or even recognize—messages he was to convey to people he didn't know? Would the voices in his mind be his own thoughts or speculations? How would he differentiate his thoughts from those coming from God?

As he pondered his situation, he wiped his mouth with his napkin and noticed his lower dentures no longer rubbed the inside of his lip, which made for a much more enjoyable meal. Then he heard sniffling and lifted his eyes to Amelia's just as she dabbed at a tear in the corner of one eye. His granddaughter was forty-three, but right now she reminded him of a young girl. Her bottom lip still trembled, and her face was flushed.

"Doodlebug, what is it?" Walter reached across the table and put a hand on hers. "It's okay if you don't believe me." He eased his hand away and shrugged. "It's hard for me to take in too."

More tears gathered in her beautiful sapphire eyes, just like her grandmother's. "How-how did everyone look? Grandma? Momma? All of them?"

Walter smiled. "Young, healthy, and beautiful."

His Doodlebug—a nickname she'd been given due to her love of the roly-poly bugs when she was little—covered her face with her hands and wept quietly.

"Don't be sad. I know you miss all those who have gone home ahead of us. I do too." Walter recalled how lovely his wife and daughter were in Heaven, and a small dagger pierced his heart as he struggled to recapture the love he'd felt in Mary Grace's arms. Even more so, in the presence of God. "But we will see them again."

Amelia uncovered her face when her phone vibrated on the table. She quickly reached for it but not before Walter saw the name 'Michael' flash across the screen. He gingerly touched his gold-rimmed glasses, which were folded in his shirt pocket and apparently not necessary anymore. He had put the glasses in his pocket when they'd left the hospital, but he hadn't needed them to read the menu.

"Hey," Amelia said softly as she chewed her bottom lip. "Did you get my message about Grandpa?" She waited, and even though Walter had an ear peeled, he couldn't hear his great-grandson's voice. "Yeah, he seems fine."

Walter wondered if Michael's troubles stemmed from not having his father in his life. Amelia and her husband had divorced when Michael was only six, and Trevor rarely saw the boy. At his core, Walter believed the kid to be a good person. A thoughtful young man who had fallen in with the wrong crowd. Walter prayed for the boy constantly. And for his mother, who had never remarried. Amelia's life revolved around her job as an administrative assistant at an oil company and bailing

Michael out of one jam or another. Walter closed his eyes and prayed for a message to give his granddaughter, something to lighten her load, but he didn't hear anything. He wondered if he ever would since that part of his story felt remote. But if anyone needed to give their problems to God, it was Amelia. She was a beautiful woman inside and out, but Walter had never been sure where she stood in her faith. Although today she had given him the impression that she did believe in an afterlife when she inquired as to how everyone in Heaven looked.

"Grandpa, I have to go." She sighed before she took a sip of water.

"Is everything okay?" Walter tried to capture her eyes, but she avoided his as she put her phone away. He had his answer.

"I'm sorry to cut things short. Michael . . ." She pressed her mouth closed, then took a deep breath. "I just need to get home. Do you want to get some red velvet cake to go?"

Walter shook his head. "I think I'll just sit here for a spell, let that steak settle, then decide if I want dessert. I'll take a cab home in a bit."

Amelia didn't like it that he took taxis to get around Houston, but when the Department of Public Safety took away his license, he didn't have a choice. He couldn't pass the eye exam. Amelia wasn't always available to drive him around, nor did he want her to have to, so he hailed a cab when he needed a ride. There was a new form of transportation called Uber, but he hadn't tried that yet.

A new thought surfaced. He could probably pass the eye exam now, but he'd sold his car over a year ago.

Perhaps he would be in the market for a new vehicle soon and regain some of his independence.

His granddaughter stood and stared at him. "Grandpa . . ." The hint of a smile lit up her face. "I've been talking softly to you, in a normal voice, ever since we left the hospital." She leaned closer and looked at one side of his face.

Walter touched his ears and realized he had forgotten to put his hearing aids in, which wasn't unusual. *Another gift from Heaven*. He gleamed back at her. "And I've heard every word you said. I won't be needing those annoying hearing aids anymore."

"That's amazing." Amelia tipped her head slightly and smiled a little more. "I'm glad today wasn't your day to go."

Walter had longed to stay in Heaven, but he also loved his earthy family, and God had assured him that he would go back someday. "Me too."

She leaned down and kissed him on the forehead. "I'll call you tonight."

Amelia called most nights around six o'clock. She reminded him to take his medicine and to check his calendar for any appointments the following day. Usually, there wasn't anything on the agenda. Maybe a doctor's appointment or an occasional coffee with his old partner at the engineering firm they'd owned and sold twenty years ago.

"I love you, Grandpa," she said before she waved and started toward the exit of the steakhouse.

"I love you, too, Doodlebug."

She moved swiftly and probably didn't hear him. He

glanced at the money on the table. Somehow, she always managed to leave money for the meal even though Walter had told her repeatedly that he had plenty of money—enough to last his entire lifetime, which was suddenly in question. How long exactly would that be? Would he have to lose his hearing and sight again? Would all his ailments slowly return? Surely the Lord wouldn't put him through more heart attacks, cancer, and the like. He scratched his chin as he wondered if he would wake up tomorrow morning and realize this had all been a dream.

Then he heard a deep and unmistakable voice in his head. *You will know him when you see him*, God said in his mind. Not only had this day not been a dream, but Walter had just been given his first message to be delivered to a man outside the restaurant. But Walter didn't move for a few minutes as he wondered if he had heard the message incorrectly. The rest of the message didn't seem to make much sense. *The blue house is not the answer, and neither is Sheila's way. Seek comfort in the house of the Lord.*

∼

Jacob stared at the dirty pavement as he leaned against the outer wall of a restaurant that he could never afford to eat in. At least the owner or one of the staff hadn't come out and asked him to move along like they'd done in the past. He seemed to have the best luck snagging leftovers from people who left the fancy steakhouse, as opposed to fast-food-type places where folks didn't usually have leftovers. Maybe the steakhouse people gave him food because they

THE MESSENGER - CHAPTER ONE

had plenty of money, or maybe it was because of the way he looked, and they just wanted him to move along.

Most days, his wavy brown hair was dirty and matted from sleeping wherever he could find a place to lay his head. He had two shirts he alternated, and occasionally he got away with rinsing them off in the fountain in front of the bank nearby, although he'd been run off from that spot too.

Never in his life would he have considered dumpster diving for food until three months ago. It was always a last resort, but hunger had a way of pushing a person's limits. Today, he was hoping for a sympathetic soul to offer him some leftovers, something more than a few French fries and part of a burger from a kid's happy meal he'd found atop a trashcan.

He'd spent a lot of time dreaming up legal ways to change his situation, but every option required the one thing he didn't have. Money. It was at the root of everything, evil or not. It bought food to nourish the body, clothed a person, and helped a guy look respectful enough to land a job, which could lead to a roof over his head. Jacob had never stolen anything in his life, but desperation caused him to put it on the agenda for later tonight. He had a plan for this evening, and no one would get hurt. Someday, he'd try to repay whatever he stole.

He looked up every time someone left the restaurant, but only two women exited carrying to-go bags, and they avoided him like the leper he was. It was two in the afternoon. He'd missed the lunch crowd. He wished he could come back closer to dinnertime. People seemed more generous at night. Maybe because they were boozed up and wanted to feel good about themselves. Jacob wasn't sure, but his mouth watered at the thought of leftover steak, chicken, pasta . . . or any other offerings on the menu. But he had just enough money in his pocket to take a cab ride to the blue house later. Then he could buy all the food he wanted.

When it came to people who drank, it seemed to go one way or the other—overly generous or out of control. When his stepfather, Leo, was riding the vodka train, the man didn't feel good about himself and didn't see anything good about Jacob. In Leo's defense, he'd been a decent stepfather until Jacob's mother died. He'd even paid for Jacob to enroll in some online college classes, citing that at twenty-two, it was time to settle on a career, or to at least start thinking about his future. Jacob had mostly held a string of jobs that weren't leading to anything that would classify as a career.

After Jacob's mother died, Leo spiraled into a depression and started knocking Jacob around, blaming him for his mother's death. And he was right. Jacob might as well have slit her wrists himself. He'd certainly driven her to it. He'd been in jail twice for driving drunk, and he'd also been arrested for disorderly conduct. He deserved the life he was living, but he couldn't take it anymore. Jacob would need to either rob the blue house in his old neighborhood where no one was ever home at night, or join his mom in the grave. He was beginning to care less and less about which option won out.

READ THE REST OF THE MESSENGER ON AMAZON.

READING GROUP GUIDE

1. Was there a point in the story when you began to suspect what Janelle was hiding from Thomas?

2. Metaphorically, what are some comparisons between Janelle and the actual Monarchs that returned each year?

3. Sometimes life unfolds in ways we cannot predict. How did God guide Janelle and Thomas onto the paths that led to their romance?

4. Have you known someone like Janelle, perhaps with a secret and struggling to love herself?

5. Janelle and her mother had a close relationship. Did you have a favorite scene that involved a conversation between the two women?

6. If you could change any part of the story, what would it be . . . and why?

AMISH RECIPES

Old Fashioned Apple Crisp
8 large applies, peeled and sliced
1 tsp. cinnamon
1 cup sugar
1 cup brown sugar
1 tsp. baking powder
1 egg
1 cup flour
1/2 tsp. salt
1/2 cup melted butter

Place the sliced apples in a 9x13x2 inch (greased) baking dish. Combine cinnamon and brown sugar. Sprinkle apples with half of the mixture. Combine sugar, flour, egg, salt, and baking powder. Spread over apple slices. Sprinkle the rest of the brown sugar and cinnamon over contents. Pour melted butter over the top. Bake at 350 for 45 minutes or until done.

Green Bean Special
2 qt. canned string beans, drained
6 oz. cream cheese
10 strips of bacon, fried and crumbled

Heat beans and drain. Add cream cheese and cover until melted. Stir in crumbled bacon and enjoy!

Ham and Cheddar Cheese Turnovers
1 17.3 oz. jumbo frig. Biscuits
2 cups ham, chopped
1 cup shredded cheddar cheese
2 T. Mustard

Shape biscuits into 6" squares and fill with hame and cheese. Moisten edges with water, press together, then bake according to package directions.

Chicken Lasagna
6 lasagna noodles (cooked)
1 can cream of chicken soup
1 can cream of mushroom
1 medium onion, chopped
1/2 cup parmesan cheese, grated
1/2 cup sour cream
1/4 cup mayonnaise
1/4 t. Garlic salt
4 cups cooked chicken
1 cup cheddar cheese
1 cup mozzarella cheese

Mix all ingredients except noodles and grated cheese. Put one layer of chicken mixture in 9x13 inch pan, then three lasagna noodles, then grated cheese. Repeat, and bake at 375 for 45 minutes.

ACKNOWLEDGMENTS

I continue to thank God for each and every story He lays upon my heart.

A huge thank you to my editors (and dear friends) Janet Murphy and Audrey Wick for the time they spent getting this story ready for publication. I couldn't do it without you gals. Love you both.

To my friends and family, thank you for your continued support as I travel on this amazing journey. Special thanks to my husband, Patrick, for his "help" with this book. Love you, Dear.

A big thank you to my street team—Wiseman's Warriors. Many of you have been with me a long time! I appreciate all of you and the time you spend helping me get the word out about my books.

I try to write stories that entertain and inspire. Thank you dear readers for trusting me with your time.

ABOUT THE AUTHOR

Bestselling and award-winning author Beth Wiseman has sold over 2.5 million books. She is the recipient of the coveted Holt Medallion, a two-time Carol Award winner, and has won the Inspirational Reader's Choice Award three times. Her books have been on various bestseller lists, including CBD, CBA, ECPA, and *Publishers Weekly*. Beth and her husband are empty nesters enjoying country life in south central Texas.

Printed in Great Britain
by Amazon